TARTS & TURNOVERS

BOOK 4 IN THE PAWS & PASTRIES SERIES

BARBARA HINSKE

CASA DEL NORTHERN PUBLISHING

ALSO BY BARBARA HINSKE

Available at Amazon in Print, Audio, and for Kindle

The Rosemont Series

Coming to Rosemont

Weaving the Strands

Uncovering Secrets

Drawing Close

Bringing Them Home

Shelving Doubts

Restoring What Was Lost

No Matter How Far

When Dreams There Be

Waves of Grace

Novellas

The Night Train

The Christmas Club (adapted

for The Hallmark Channel, 2019)

Paws & Pastries

Sweets & Treats

Snowflakes, Cupcakes & Kittens

Tarts & Turnovers

Workout Wishes & Valentine Kisses

Wishes of Home

Wishful Tails

Back in the Pack

CONNECT WITH BARBARA HINSKE ONLINE

Sign up for her newsletter at **BarbaraHinske.com**
    Goodreads.com/BarbaraHinske
    Facebook/bhinske
    Instagram/barbarahinskeauthor
    TikTok.com/BarbaraHinske
    Pinterest.com/BarbaraHinske
    X.com/BarbaraHinske
    Search for **Barbara Hinske on YouTube**
    bhinske@gmail.com

TARTS & TURNOVERS

Tarts & Turnovers by Barbara Hinske

This book may not be reproduced in whole or in part without written permission of the author, with the exception of brief quotations within book reviews or articles. This book is a work of fiction. Any resemblance to actual persons, living or dead, or places or events is coincidental.

ISBN: 9798991115124

LCCN: 2024921739

Casa del Northern Publishing

Phoenix, Arizona

To all the gal pals who have listened to my dreams, helped me navigate challenges, and supported me on life's journey. Women have a unique capacity to bond, and I'm profoundly grateful for it.

CHAPTER 1

The lights flickered, then shut off completely, plunging Sweets & Treats into the late-afternoon gloom of a rainy day. A frisson of fear skittered down Clara's spine. She'd paid the electric bill for the patisserie on the last day for payment listed on the disconnect notice. Surely the utility company hadn't shut off her service by mistake.

She walked to the display window at the front of her shop she'd opened a few months earlier. Water spilled from the gutters, mirroring the effect of a wall-of-water-type fountain she'd seen in the lobby of a hotel. Lights were off in the shops across the street. Clara forced her jaw to unclench. The storm must have been responsible for the power outage.

Clara opened the weather app on her phone. The radar map showed a solid band of thunderstorms across the entire state. The chance of rain for the rest of the week was listed at 100% every day.

She scanned her display case. The man who owned the guitar store next to Sweets & Treats had been her only customer of the day. He'd stopped in before he opened his store for coffee and a chocolate croissant.

Rows of colorful macarons snaked from the front of the case to the back. Next came sugar cookies decorated to look like flowers, ladybugs, smiley faces, and watermelons. Cupcakes in six flavors—including the July flavor of the month, lemon meringue—stood where she'd placed them before she'd opened the shop. The next case showcased croissants, cinnamon rolls, and cherry Danish.

The baskets in the wire rack behind the case held French baguettes, cinnamon-raisin cottage loaves, and gruyere-stuffed crusty loaves. Her staff had baked all night and none of what they'd made had sold.

"The kitchen is cleaned up and I sent the staff home." Her senior baker came to stand with her. Joan rested her hand on Clara's shoulder. "It's been raining cats and dogs the entire day. No one's going to come out on an afternoon like this."

Clara continued to stare out the window. "I know," she finally replied. "We only had one customer today. Monday and Tuesday weren't much better. I'm losing my shirt this week."

"I cut back our offerings, like you said," Joan said, a note of defensiveness in her voice.

"I know you did, Joan." Clara scanned the cases behind them. "We have to provide a selection for customers. We're still making a name for ourselves. I can't have someone stop in first thing in the morning to find our shelves bare."

"I agree. That sends the wrong message."

"I knew when I opened this patisserie that the average bakery loses money for the first three years." She gave Joan a rueful smile. "I didn't believe my patisserie would be average."

"And it's *not* average. We had a terrific spring. Remember Easter week? We turned out so many lamb cakes, croissants, and macarons, I swear we could have gone for the Guinness World Record."

The corners of Clara's lips twitched upwards. "That was an amazing week. Everyone worked so hard." Clara's voice grew thick with emotion. "I've got the best baking staff on the planet." She blinked rapidly. "That's why days like today are so discouraging. I don't want to lose any of you."

"Do you need to lay someone off?"

Clara shook her head. "Not yet. I budgeted for slow times, and I have reserves. Until now, the bad days have been interspersed between days where we at least break even. Looking at the weather forecast"—she held up her phone—"I think we'll lose money the entire week."

Clara pointed to the clock on the wall above the register. "It's ten minutes until quitting time. Let's box everything up. Take home as much as you want."

"Thank you. Hungry teenagers will blow through a lot of this, but I can't use it all. Why don't we save most of it for tomorrow?"

"No. We're building our reputation as a first-rate patisserie. That means we don't sell day-old goods." Clara's tone was stern.

"Okay, okay. Do you want to take some of this with you?"

"I'll bring a gruyere loaf, a dozen cookies, and a half-dozen cupcakes to Ian, Laura, and Tabitha. Those are their favorites. Plus, a croissant for my breakfast. The rest can go to the homeless shelter."

Joan nodded. "I'll drop them off on my way home."

"Thank you."

"I instructed the late crew to make this"—she gestured to the cases and bread racks behind her—"every night this week. Want me to cut back even further?"

Clara pursed her lips, considering the unsold product they were about to box up to give away. "No. This is the bare minimum of what we should stock." She inhaled slowly. "I'm going to have to hitch up my britches and realize we're going to be in the red this week."

"What about the bakery case Sweets & Treats has at Johanson's Diner? Do you know if they sold out of our baked goods, like usual?"

Clara's shoulders dropped a bit more. "Josef called me about an hour ago. This rain has affected their business, too. He said the case is almost full."

"I'm so sorry, Clara. This amount of rain is unusual for Pinewood."

Lightning flashed. The thunder clapped and rumbled away into the distance.

"At least we haven't had tornadoes like so many of the other cities around us," Joan said as she folded bakery boxes for herself and Clara.

"I'm thankful for that," Clara said. "Do we get them in Pinewood?"

"Not often. We've never had one here in the downtown area. A tornado touched down out by the highway, but that was years ago."

"Good," Clara said. "We can cope with the rain and a lousy revenue week."

Clara locked the front door and turned the sign to CLOSED. She and Joan boxed up the baked goods with practiced precision.

Clara set the treats for her landlady's family to one side and helped Joan carry her boxes to the trunk of her car.

"Are you leaving now, too?" Joan asked as she slammed the trunk shut.

Clara shook her head.

"Do you want me to stay?"

"No. You should head home. I'm going to cut down our order of baking supplies for next week. We'll have half of our supplies from this week left over."

"Good idea." Joan stepped to the driver's side door, rain turning her hair into a soppy mess. "Chin up," she called as she flung herself behind the wheel. "We'll survive this."

Clara waved goodbye and sprinted through the downpour to the kitchen door of her beloved—but struggling—patisserie.

CHAPTER 2

Clara started at the sharp knock on the back door of Sweets & Treats, dropping her pencil onto the papers scattered across her usually tidy desk in the corner of the workroom. She got to her feet and shuffled to the door, stiff from hunching over the spreadsheet on her laptop.

The knock came again, accompanied by a voice she knew and loved.

"Clara," Kurt Holbrook called. "It's me."

She lunged for the handle as she put her hand to her forehead. She'd completely forgotten their dinner date. Clara opened the door, saying "I'm so sorry," at the same time he was saying it.

Kurt stepped inside as the wind brought a sheet of rain with him. He pushed the door closed with his shoulder and stood on the inside doormat, a soggy pizza box in his hand. Water dripped from the brim of his baseball cap and puddled at his feet.

Clara ran her hands down the length of her baker's apron that she hadn't bothered to take off. Strands of her long, chestnut-colored hair had escaped the neat bun she'd styled at four that morning. The scant makeup she wore during the workday was long gone. She wanted her über-successful lawyer and property-owner boyfriend to see her as a successful young entrepreneur, but she was sure she looked exhausted, depressed, and worried.

"You didn't get my texts." He said it as a statement rather than a question.

"No." She ushered him inside, glancing around herself. "In fact, I don't know where my phone is."

"I wondered why you didn't reply." He set the pizza box on one of the spotlessly clean worktables and turned to her. "I texted that I needed to check on rain damage at the construction site. I planned to do it this afternoon, but I got tied up and couldn't leave my office early. I asked if you'd mind if we changed our plans. I'd pick up a pizza and bring it to your place when I was done." He gestured to the box. "You've been working so hard lately, I didn't want to cancel and leave you in the lurch for dinner."

"That's very thoughtful of you, Kurt." Clara leaned in and kissed his cheek.

"I drove by your place, but your car wasn't there, so I headed here. I was concerned something had happened to you." He ran his eyes over her. "That's clearly not the case."

She put her palms to her temples, shaking her head. "I'm not going to lie—I forgot about our plans. I've had such a lousy day and…" She raised her eyes to meet his. "That's no excuse. I'm so sorry."

"It's okay. Happens to everyone. I was excited to see you… and concerned when you weren't home."

She stepped close to him. "I'm always happy to see you," she said, placing her hands on his shoulders. "I lost track of time."

He swept her into a hug and they kissed. "Are you hungry? We have a cold sausage and pepperoni pizza with extra cheese in that box."

"Starved. The only thing I've had today is at least six cups of coffee."

"That's not good for you," Kurt admonished. "It's not like you, either."

"I know. I've been in such a funk, I didn't care." She opened the lid of the pizza box. "I can warm this up in a jiffy."

"That's not necessary on my account," Kurt said. "As a bachelor, I've acquired a taste for cold pizza."

She grinned at him. "Don't tell, but sometimes I prefer it cold."

They each perched on a stool by the table, picked up a slice of pizza, and began to eat.

"So… tell me what's got you so upset." Kurt took a bite.

"Business has been slow this summer."

"Last time we talked, you told me you were expecting that."

She nodded. "Just not this bad. I only had one sale today—one tiny sale."

Kurt grimaced. "That's brutal. It's got to be because of the rain. They're saying on the news that we're having the rainiest summer in the last fifty years."

"Lucky me." Clara covered her mouth with her hand as she talked while she chewed. "What a terrific time to open a walk-in business."

"It's just one week," Kurt said. "Surely there are things you can do to cut your losses."

"That's what I was working on when you arrived. I started right after closing time."

"What about cutting down on the selection you offer? Bakeries have it worse than restaurants because your products are even more perishable."

"We're only baking the bare minimum this week. I can't cut back any further without risking the reputation of Sweets & Treats."

He nodded, handing her another slice of pizza before he took another for himself.

"I'm overstaffed for our current production needs. Thank goodness some of my bakers are out every week for vacation. If the slowdown continues into the fall, I'll have to lay someone off." Her voice was tinged with misery.

"I understand you don't want to do that," he replied, "but you may have to. These difficult decisions are part of owning a business."

She recoiled from his words. "You think I don't know that?"

He held up both palms. "I'm not saying that."

"Do you expect the downturn to continue into the fall?" Her tone was shrill.

"No. I think things will pick up. Honestly, you're having a bad week because of the rain and you're getting worked up over things that won't happen."

"So, I'm exaggerating?"

"Sweetheart—no. I'm upsetting you and I don't want to do that. I've represented business clients for years and was only offering some perspective. All I'm trying to do is be helpful."

"Have any of your other clients owned bakeries? Do you have experience in my business? As you alluded to earlier, bakeries have special challenges."

"Nope. None. I'm sorry I said anything. I'll mind my own business from now on. Ha. Sorry about the pun."

They finished the pizza in silence.

"How are things out at your grandfather's old farmhouse? Were any of the renovations you've had done since you bought the property damaged by the storm?"

"Nope. Everything's fine." He closed the lid on the pizza box and stood.

"I'd like to hear more about the progress of the renovations," Clara said.

"That can wait. I've got an early day tomorrow—and you always have an early day. Let's find that phone of yours before I leave."

Clara got to her feet and crossed to the line of refrigerators and freezers along one wall of the workroom. "It'll be in one of these. I did a quick inventory of supplies after closing and have been calculating how much I can reduce my order for next week." She opened the doors and found her phone on a shelf inside the third unit. "I've made this mistake before." She gave Kurt a sad face. "I'm sorry I missed your texts. And forgot our dinner. And most of all, that I got so snippy with you."

He placed the pizza box in the trash and crossed to her. "Don't worry about it. You've got a lot on your mind. I admire your dedication to your business and the responsibility you feel to your employees." He opened his arms to her, and she fell into them.

"I'm going to make this patisserie a success," she mumbled into his chest.

"Of course you are. No doubt about it." He lifted her chin with his finger, and they kissed long and slow.

"Can I have a… rain check… on tonight?" she whispered.

"Sure. I'll take you anywhere you want to go for dinner on Saturday."

"I'd like you to come to my place. At 6:00."

"You don't have to cook after a long week."

"I love cooking. It's my happy place."

"Then I'll see you at six. Are you ready to get out of here?"

"Yes. I changed our supply order hours ago and was obsessively rehashing everything." Clara glanced at her desktop, strewn with papers. "Let me log off and shove those papers in a drawer. I don't want the night bakers to see any of it."

"I'll haul the trash to the dumpster and see you to your car."

She caught his hand and squeezed it. "Thank you for being so kind, Kurt. I'm lucky to have you in my life."

CHAPTER 3

*I*an Ramsey leaned his bicycle against the railing and climbed the stairs to the front door of the bungalow that sat on the other side of the town square from his grandmother's stately brick Victorian home. Houses on either side of the bungalow were imposing two-story structures.

The past week's storms had passed, and the sun struggled to reacquaint itself with the day. Shadows from the neighboring homes fell across the bungalow's porch as if they were protecting their smaller counterpart.

Maisie Johanson opened the door before Ian had the chance to ring the bell. "Good morning, Ian." She held the door wide and ushered him inside.

"Morning, Ms. Johanson," he said, stepping gingerly over the threshold.

"Before we start, I'd like to ask another favor of you." She stood in the entryway and looked into his eyes.

"Sure."

"Will you call me Maisie?"

"I don't know… my great-grandmother wouldn't like it."

"You're here today to help me refine my curriculum for my 'Cooking 101' course. I'd call that being a collaborator. In my book, that means we should be on a first-name basis." Maisie tilted her head to one side. "Tabitha is one of my dearest friends, and I'm sure she'd agree with me."

Ian shifted his weight from side to side. "Okay. If you say so."

"I do." The older woman turned toward the kitchen. "Follow me."

They entered the cozy room lined with warm pine cabinets set against lattice-work wallpaper strewn with strawberries and roses. Starched white curtains framed a large window above a farmhouse sink.

Maisie motioned him toward a chair at the kitchen table. His place had been set with cutlery, a napkin, and a glass of water. "It'll help me design my class if you do some taste testing for me." She looked at him over the top of her half-moon glasses. "Are you up for that?"

He nodded. "I can always eat."

She chuckled. "Most boys your age can. What grade are you going into next year?" She walked to the stove and turned her back to him.

"Seventh."

Maisie poured a yellow mixture into a hot pan and stirred it with a spatula. "What's your favorite subject?"

"Science. I think I want to be a veterinarian."

"Cooking is science," she said. "More specifically, it's chemistry. Are you familiar with a book called *Lessons in Chemistry*?"

"I know my mom read it for her book club."

Maisie gave the scrambled eggs in the pan one last turn and slid the pan off the hot burner, moving another non-stick pan onto it. She placed a teaspoon of a white powder into a small glass mixing bowl and added a tablespoon of water, then whisked it together. When the cornstarch had dissolved, she stirred the mixture into the remaining liquid eggs and whisked them until the eggs became frothy. She poured this mixture into the pan and began scrambling the eggs.

"I'm making scrambled eggs two different ways," she said. "The difference is slight, but noticeable. As you can see, it took no time at all." She turned off the burner. Maisie spooned the scrambled eggs from each pan onto a plate, dusted them with salt and pepper, and deposited the plate on the table in front of Ian.

"Please taste each of these scrambled eggs, taking a drink of water when you go from one batch to the other."

"I've seen them do that on the cooking shows my great-grandma watches. It's called clearing the plate—or something like that."

"Clearing the palette. That's exactly what I'd like you to do. Tell me if you notice any difference between the two groups of eggs."

Ian picked up his fork. "This one is bigger and taller." He touched the tines to the top of one mound of egg.

"It is. That's excellent. You can tell a lot about food by the way it looks. You need to use all five senses when you cook."

"It's not only taste?"

"That's the main one, but others are essential to being an accomplished cook." She slid into the chair across from him. "What else?"

He took a forkful from one mound of eggs and chewed it slowly, then took a drink of water and ate a bite from the other egg. Ian narrowed his eyes in thought, then repeated the process.

Maisie waited patiently for his response.

"This one—the taller stack—is lighter and fluffier."

"That's right!" Maisie slapped the tabletop with her palm in delight. "Why do you think that is?"

"Did you put that white stuff in this one and beat it with the whisk?"

"Right again. That white stuff is corn starch. I mixed it into water to make a starchy slurry and added it to the liquid eggs. A starchy slurry prevents scrambled eggs from setting up too firmly. Corn starch kept them tender and moist."

"That's cool."

"As I said, that's chemistry."

"I've never seen my mom or great-grandma do that."

"I'll let you practice it here before you go home. Surprise your mom and Tabitha with the best scrambled eggs they've ever had."

"That'd be fun." He finished eating the eggs on his plate. "Are there other tricks like that with cooking?"

"Yes. There are plenty of simple techniques and skills that elevate everyday meals to something special. You don't need an enormous kitchen, expensive equipment, or extravagant ingredients to be an exceptional cook. Mastering the basics is where it starts." Her enthusiasm for her subject surged from her like an ocean at high tide.

"So scrambling eggs will be one lesson?"

Maisie nodded. "I'll also go over ways to use cornstarch or other ingredients to thicken gravies or sauces. I'm trying to decide if I should focus my lessons on a particular meal, or a particular technique."

"Like when you showed me how to use a knife?"

"Exactly. I want my students to take home a meal for their family after every class. The knife skills lesson will revolve around a main dish salad." She looked into his eyes. "Be honest. Does that sound interesting?"

He nodded emphatically. "I already asked my mom if I can sign up for the first class. She said definitely."

Maisie grinned and picked up a spiral-bound notebook from the table. "I've made notes and have questions for you. As I said, your answers will help me organize this class. I want it to be a success so I can keep teaching." She whipped her glasses off of her face. "I know this sounds silly, but I firmly believe that people lead calmer and more fulfilling lives when they've got a lovely meal in their stomachs." She perched her glasses back on her nose. "No one is ever at their best when they're hangry. My mission is to eliminate hangriness—and cooking mediocrity—by teaching people how to be remarkable home cooks."

CHAPTER 4

Kurt turned off the state highway onto a road that zigzagged along a ridge and deposited him at the gravel track leading to the familiar farmhouse he now owned. The sun had just cleared the horizon. After a week of non-stop rain, the lush vegetation was greener and more robust than he'd ever seen.

He rolled down his windows, the crisp air whipping past his ears. Kurt inhaled deeply, as if he were quenching a great thirst. The property was only thirty minutes outside of Pinewood, but he felt as if he was in another world. The tensions of his lawyer career melted away like butter on hot biscuits. Buying his grandparent's old place as a second home was one of the best purchases he'd ever made.

Kurt pulled up to the newly graded driveway leading to the house. Once paved, it would provide access to suppliers who could deposit construction materials behind the house instead of leaving them along the road. The rain had delayed the asphalt company's progress.

The delivery of the bathroom tile for the expanded upstairs bathroom and the new downstairs powder room had been scheduled for that Saturday morning—to the curb. Kurt had worried that the pallets of costly specialty tile would "walk away" if left at the side of the road unattended all weekend. Instead, he'd collected the tile from the supplier and planned to drive it up to the house. Now that he was here, he wasn't sure he'd be successful.

He sat in his truck, staring out at a muddy track where an asphalt driveway should have been. He got out and walked up the incline toward the house, testing the integrity of the unfinished driveway. The lug soles of his work boots sunk into a half inch of mud before connecting with a solid surface. His four-wheel drive could handle this. He'd be able to deliver his cargo of tile to the door.

Kurt urged his truck along the driveway and parked in the driest patch he could find near the back door. He contemplated using his two-wheel cart to ferry the boxes of tile into the house, but decided pulling it across the uneven terrain would be more trouble than it was worth. He'd carry the boxes inside.

By the time Kurt had finished lugging the heavy boxes across the yard, up the steps, and into the hallway outside the small first-floor powder room, his shirt was wet with perspiration and his muscles were talking to him. He worked out at the gym every day, he muttered to himself. Why was carrying tile so difficult?

He contemplated leaving the installation for the crew, who would return on Monday to finish the bathrooms. Given the stiffness in his lower back, that would have been the sensible thing to do. But he had planned to invite Clara for a picnic on Sunday to see the progress that had been made on the renovation, and he wanted her to see the tile she'd helped him select laid down in at least one bathroom.

Kurt set to work with singular focus. He installed the floor tile in the powder room and created a baseboard using it. Everything went smoothly, with only a handful of tiles requiring cuts. He stood in the doorway to the tiny room, admiring his handiwork. The hexagons of white tile were punctuated at regular intervals with small black diamond-shaped tiles. The overall effect was timeless and elegant. What had the salesperson said? This tile would bring a modern sensibility to a classic look. He wasn't sure what that meant, but he knew he loved the way the floor looked and was eager to show it to Clara.

Kurt placed his hands at the small of his back and stretched from side to side. Earlier that morning, he'd considered installing the upstairs bathroom floor, too. As he trudged up the stairs, he abandoned that idea. Home improvements looked easy on television, but doing them in real life was another story.

He turned to his left at the top of the stairs and checked on the bedroom on that side of the house. Originally, there had been two bedrooms, but he'd turned one of them into an addition to the minuscule upstairs bath. The hardwood floors in the bedroom had been sanded and refinished, and glowed in the soft sunshine streaming through the windows. The walls and ceiling had been painted a warm off-white with the cheerful name of crème brûlée. He chuckled as he remembered Clara's childlike enthusiasm for the color, based almost entirely on the name. This room was move-in ready.

He shut the door and crossed the hallway to the bedroom on the other side that ran the length of the house. Still small by modern standards, the large double-hung windows and intricately detailed baseboards and crown molding gave the room an air of elegance and importance. The wood floors in this room had also been refinished, but he'd restored the baseboards and crown molding himself. It had been a painstaking labor of love, but he'd enjoyed every moment of the work. His grandfather had made both of the baseboards and molding in his shop in the barn as a surprise birthday present for his grandmother. Kurt had felt their presence when he'd been sanding and scraping, staining and finishing—as if they were still alive.

Their marriage had been the lifelong love he'd always wanted

—and thought he'd found with Maisie and Josef's daughter Rachel. All three of them had been devastated when she died of cancer years ago. Kurt had gone to a dark place then—certain he'd never love again.

Maisie and Josef hadn't allowed him to succumb to despair. They'd taken him into their generous hearts and helped him heal. They'd insisted he'd find a loving partner again and had encouraged and rejoiced in his relationship with Clara.

He noticed the closet door stood ajar and he crossed the room to close it. The top of the door caught on something sticking out from the top shelf. He'd spent hours working in this room and never noticed anything in the closet.

He strained to reach the top shelf and pulled out a weathered manilla envelope. The wavering handwriting on the front was his grandmother's, in her later years. She'd scrawled the words "Favorite Family Photos" across the middle of the envelope.

Kurt took it to the window and bent the old metal tabs to release the closure. The old metal, weak with age, broke off in his hands. He raised the flap and withdrew a handful of old photographs. One was of his grandparents as a young couple, standing in their Sunday best in front of this very house. He flipped it over and noted the date on the back. It was taken the spring after his grandfather had built the house.

Kurt felt a lump form in his throat. They would have been fifteen years younger than he was now.

The next photo showed them with their four young children. Two boys and two girls. Three of them died of polio. His father was the only one who had lived into adulthood. The lump grew bigger.

Birthdays, baptisms, and the occasional Christmas had been photographed and recorded—all in this house.

The last photo was also taken outside—on the front porch. Of more recent vintage than the rest, it showed his parents, sitting on a wooden porch swing, holding a toddler between them. The child was him.

Kurt stared at the photo. He remembered that swing. He'd loved it. His grandparents had allowed him to play on it for hours. It had been a pirate ship, a fire engine, a horse, and a dump truck. He smiled as he thought of the buckets of sand he'd sent flying off that swing when it had been a dump truck. Tears pricked the backs of his eyes. His meticulously clean grandmother must have hated the mess he created, but she'd never scolded him. Both of his grandparents had encouraged his interests without reservations.

He blinked the dampness from his eyes and placed the photos back in the envelope. He'd take them to show Clara that night.

He checked his watch. He needed to hightail it home if he was going to get the shower he needed and be at Clara's by 6:00.

Kurt raced down the stairs, gathered his tools, and headed for his truck. He placed them in the cab and stopped before he swung himself into the driver's seat. He needed to check something.

He clomped through the overgrown grass to the front of the house and climbed the steps to the front porch. The swing had been gone for decades. He searched the ceiling of the porch and found what he was looking for: iron eyebolts. He reached up and examined them. They were still securely in place and showed no traces of rust. The surrounding wood was in fine shape.

"I'll replace the swing," he promised his grandparents, tilting his head back and speaking to the heavens.

Kurt hopped off the porch and whistled as he made his way back to his truck. He couldn't wait to keep that promise.

Noelle rose onto her haunches in the window seat of the cottage. Nestled into the trees behind the stately red-brick Victorian where Ian and Laura lived with Laura's grandmother, Tabitha Trent, it was a charming miniature version of the main house. Clara had leased it from them when she'd moved to Pinewood and she and her pup, Noelle, had settled into the cottage and welcoming community with ease.

The dachshund/terrier mix pressed her nose into the glass and her hindquarters swayed like a small boat in high seas as she watched the figure approach on the long flagstone walkway from the big house to the cottage. As he got closer, her excitement swelled and she emitted a series of welcoming woofs.

Clara stepped out of the kitchen, drying her hands on a towel. "Is that him, girl?" she asked in a sing-song voice. "Your favorite person in the world, next to me?"

Noelle kept her focus on Kurt, now only a few strides from the door.

"Or maybe you like Kurt better than me?" Clara gave her beloved terrier mix a quick pat as she walked past on her way to the door. "Not that I'd blame you. He sneaks you table scraps and brings you toys every time he comes."

Clara opened the door as Kurt raised his hand to knock.

He stepped inside. "I guess your early warning system alerted you I was coming." He held out an enormous bouquet of blue and pink hydrangeas.

"These are stunning," she said, taking them from him and leaning in to kiss him.

"They're from my grandparent's property," he said. "The bushes are huge."

"Hydrangeas are my favorite summer flower. I'd love to see them." She crossed to a bookcase flanking the living room fireplace and removed a crystal vase. "I'll put these in water while you give Noelle her gifts." She smiled at him as the dog sat at his feet, tail sweeping the carpet and eyes glued to him.

Kurt grinned sheepishly. "How do you know I've got something for her?"

"How do I know the sun will come up every day?" Clara's voice trailed off as she went into the kitchen.

Kurt dropped to one knee to greet Noelle. "Your mommy's so smart, isn't she?"

Noelle uttered a single yip.

"I *do* have something for you." He reached into the back pocket of his jeans and brought out a small squeaky toy in the shape of a ladybug.

Noelle jumped to her feet.

Kurt pressed the toy to make it squeak, then threw it across the room and into the hallway.

Noelle was after it in a flash. After squeezing it a few times in her mouth, she brought it back to Kurt, and he threw it for her until Clara returned with the flowers in the vase.

She set it on the mantel and stood back to admire the arrangement. "They couldn't be prettier," she said. "Thank you for bringing them to me."

"My pleasure. You can pick more tomorrow if you want. Would you like to join me for a picnic at my grandparent's home?"

"I'd love that! It's supposed to be another beautiful day. Can I pick a big bunch for Tabitha? Her arthritis has flared, and she's practically housebound. These will cheer her up."

"Then it's a date. I'll pick you up at 11:00. I can't wait to show you the progress on the renovation. And I'd like to get your advice on the kitchen layout. The designer's given me three different scenarios and I can't decide between them. Since you actually cook—as opposed to warming up takeout, like me—I'd value your opinion."

"That sounds like the perfect day to me. There's just one thing we need to do before we go out there." Her tone was serious.

He stood to face her. "What's that?"

"You can't keep calling it your grandparent's house. It's yours, now. I'll bet they're watching down on you and are thrilled with the changes you're making."

Kurt shrugged. "I call it that because it sounds pretentious to call it my second home or my vacation home…"

Clara led him through the kitchen to an ornamental iron bistro table in her back garden. A vintage round tablecloth decorated with morning glories covered it, and two places were set with china and crystal. An open bottle of red wine stood in the middle, breathing. She poured them each a glass and handed one to him.

"I think you should give the house its own name."

"Like Downton Abbey?" His eyes twinkled as he mentioned her favorite show. "Isn't the place a bit too small for a name of its own?"

"Size has nothing to do with it."

He took a sip of his wine as he considered this. "Hilltop House?"

"Hmmm…. That's a bit bland." Clara swirled her wine in her glass. "How about Bloom Cottage?"

Kurt nodded. "I like it. If you looked at the place right now, you'd agree with the name."

"It's charming and cozy, but slightly feminine, too. Does that bother you?"

"Nah. Everything about the place is warm and welcoming. Its name has to reflect that."

"To Bloom Cottage." Clara raised her glass in a toast.

"To Bloom Cottage," Kurt repeated, clinking her glass.

They each took a sip of their wine.

"Are you hungry?" Clara asked.

"Starved. I worked at my grand… no, Bloom Cottage the entire day and didn't stop for lunch. What're we having?" He lifted his chin a fraction of an inch and sniffed the air.

"You noticed how clean the kitchen was as we walked through?"

"Now that you mention it, yes."

"I was slammed at Sweets & Treats today," she said. "So much so that Joan and I baked extra cookies during every spare moment."

"That's fabulous news! People must have been waiting for the weather to clear up."

"It appears so. For the first time in more than a week, we sold out of everything. I even got orders for two birthday cakes and three dozen cupcakes for a baby shower."

"I'm so happy for you." He swept her into a hug.

"Unfortunately, I didn't get out of the bakery in time to pick up groceries and rustle up a meal."

"Shall I take us out?"

She shook her head. "I stopped at Johanson's Diner and got us each a meal I knew we'd like. All I had to do was set the table."

She put her glass on the table. "Have a seat and I'll bring out our meals."

He lowered himself into a chair.

"In case you're wondering," Clara said, over her shoulder, "I'm having a mixed green salad with seared ahi tuna, and you're having a full rack of Josef's spareribs."

She felt, rather than saw, the smile that erupted on his face.

CHAPTER 6

Kurt and Clara sipped coffee as they destroyed the cherry cheesecake cupcakes with dark chocolate ganache icing she'd brought home for dessert.

"I can't believe you had any of these left to bring home," Kurt said, licking the last bit of icing from his fork. "Every time I try something else that you've baked, I think it's the best thing I've ever had."

Clara's cheeks turned the same rosy pink as the cupcakes. "I put two of them aside before we opened or we wouldn't be having dessert. I'm glad you like them. The recipe is new, and I wanted to see how well it did today."

"You're a baking genius." He eyed the half cupcake that sat untouched on her plate.

She caught his eye and pushed the plate toward him. "Would you like to finish this?"

"I don't want to take it from you." The look in his eyes belied his words.

Clara laughed. "I taste test all day long at the bakery. By the time I get home, I've had enough. You're more than welcome to it."

He devoured the cupcake in two bites, scraping the plate for every last crumb.

"You really like that, don't you?"

"Uh… yeah!"

"Should I make it my cupcake of the week, next week?"

"Absolutely. I'm preordering two dozen right here and now to take to the office on Tuesday."

"You don't have to do that."

"I want to. They're fabulous. Besides, you know I support my tenants. It's in my personal interest to make sure you succeed."

"Speaking of tenants, did you know that Nick Sutherland is hosting an open mic night at the guitar store?"

"He does that once a quarter. It gives his guitar students a chance to perform in a low-stress setting."

"Nick's a nice next-door neighbor. He stops in every morning for his coffee and invited me personally to stop by tonight."

"That was nice of him. Do you want to go for a little while?"

She nodded. "Unless you're too tired. You've had a long day."

"Like you haven't? It's a beautiful evening. Let's walk. It'll be nice to stretch our legs after this wonderful dinner."

"Can we take Noelle with us? She didn't get her usual walks on the rainy days. Ian texted that he was tied up with Maisie the entire day and I didn't get home in time to take her. She's been cooped up in the house for a week."

Kurt reached under the table to pat the dog, who lay curled at their feet. "Of course she can. Nick keeps a water bowl by the door of his shop for his canine customers."

"Wanna go for a walk?" Clara directed the question to Noelle.

The dog leapt to her feet and raced into the house.

They picked up their dessert plates and coffee cups and followed Noelle inside.

"Leave these in the sink," Clara said. "I'll be up at dawn since I can't master the art of sleeping in and will deal with cleanup then."

She snapped the leash on her squirming dog, and they stepped out into the balmy evening. The sky was losing the final streaks of pink and purple as the prolonged summer dusk gave way to night. Fireflies put on a light show underneath the canopy of the trees while they traversed the short distance, hand in hand, to the shop adjoining Sweets & Treats.

Light from the guitar store's display window spilled onto the sidewalk in front. The door was open wide. As they got close, they heard the complicated ending of a flamenco piece, followed by a smattering of enthusiastic applause.

They slipped inside as an older man relinquished the stool in front of the microphone to a young woman wearing a T-shirt emblazoned with the local university's logo.

At six foot four, Kurt didn't sneak in anywhere. Nick saw his friend and landlord and, after introducing the young woman to the crowd, crossed the room to welcome them.

"Thank you for the cookies you sent over this afternoon," he whispered to Clara. "They've been a big hit."

Clara smiled. "Of course."

A Golden Retriever with a white muzzle and a calm demeanor appeared at Nick's side.

Noelle leaned forward to sniff the other dog—her tail wagging kicked into overdrive.

Nick pointed to the door and led the big dog outside.

Noelle was right behind them, and Kurt and Clara followed along.

"Best to let these two make friends out here," Nick said. "We don't want to disturb the performers."

The old dog allowed Noelle to perform a thorough inspection.

"We shouldn't have brought Noelle inside," Clara said. "I don't want to disrupt your evening."

"You're doing no such thing," Nick said. "Jack likes his new friend. I can tell. What's her name, again?"

"Noelle."

"Hello, Noelle," he said, bending over to introduce himself to Clara's dog. "Do you come to work like Jack does every day with me?"

"Gosh, no," Clara said. "She's not a service dog, so she shouldn't be in a bakery."

"That's too bad. I love having Jack with me. Particularly on slow days. He's a terrific companion, even if he spends most of his time asleep on the memory foam bed in the corner. Customers love him."

Clara knelt and gave the friendly dog a rub down. "I can see why."

"How'd you do last week?" Nick asked. "If I'm not being too nosey."

Clara stood. "I lost my shirt Monday through Friday. Today was busy, so that helped, but I barely broke even for the week."

He nodded. "Same here. Summer is always slow in the downtown area. Last week's rain added insult to injury." He gave her a rueful smile. "Hang in there. I know how tough it is to run a small retail business, especially when you're getting started. It takes time to make a name for yourself. Things pick up for me when school starts up in the fall. I'm sure they will for you, too."

Jack lay on the concrete at his master's feet and sprawled on his side. Noelle nestled herself against him.

"I sure hope so," Clara said. "We're trying out new products constantly to figure out what our customers want."

"Keep it up," he said. "You'll be successful." He tilted his head toward his shoulder. "May I suggest something?"

"Of course."

"Why don't we post notices in each other's shops? Give me your menu—lists of daily specials—whatever you'd like. I'll provide notices about lessons, open mic nights like this one, and my semi-annual sales."

"That's a great idea," Clara said.

"I've tried in the past to get the downtown merchants to collaborate—without much success. There are lots of examples in other communities where joint efforts have been beneficial."

"I agree with you. Who knows"—she flashed him her megawatt smile—"maybe the two of us can get something started."

"You're on." Nick extended his hand to her, and they shook on it.

Applause erupted from inside his shop. "That's my cue. I'd better get inside to introduce the next player." He looked down at Jack and Noelle—both snoring softly.

"One more thing," he said, reaching down to wake Jack. "You're welcome to bring Noelle with you any day that I'm open and leave her with Jack and me. We'd love to have her."

He and Jack made their way to the microphone.

"Look at you, Noelle, making friends," Clara said.

"Would you like to go inside again to listen to music?"

Clara answered with a yawn that spread to Kurt and then Noelle.

"We're all bushed," Kurt said. "Let's get you home."

Clara rested her forehead against his chest and nodded. "I've hit the wall, I'm afraid. I'll get a solid night's sleep and be ready to help you plan the new kitchen at Bloom Cottage tomorrow."

CHAPTER 7

Clara slipped into the front pew next to Josef thirty seconds before the pastor gave the invocation.

He glanced over and winked at her.

Clara smiled at him in return as she relaxed into her seat. She scanned the choir and found Maisie in her usual place in the alto section. Their eyes met and Maisie nodded to her.

She bowed her head for the opening prayer and succumbed to the peace that the prayers, music, and message of the Sunday service inevitably brought her. The last chords of the closing hymn faded, and she stood, feeling centered in her thoughts and refreshed in her spirit.

Josef turned to her, and they hugged before filing out of the pew. She inched along behind him in the line to greet their pastor, admiring the way Josef interacted with those in his path. Everyone he encountered knew and loved the older man.

He turned to her after they'd each shaken the pastor's hand and moved into the swell of people congregating outside the sanctuary. "It was nice to see you here this morning."

"I'm glad I came. I always feel better when I do, but I've been so busy getting Sweets & Treats off the ground that I haven't had time." She glanced up at him. "Or—rather—made the time."

"Will you come to the coffee hour? I'm not the only person around here who's missed you."

Clara shook her head. "Kurt's picking me up soon. We're taking a picnic lunch out to Bloom Cottage. He wants me to see the renovations and get my thoughts on his kitchen layout."

"Bloom Cottage?"

Clara chuckled. "We named it that last night. I told him he needs to stop calling it his grandparent's house."

"I knew his grandparents well. They'd approve."

"Who'd approve of what?"

Josef and Clara turned to see Maisie approaching them, her choir robe engulfing her petite frame.

Clara filled her in.

Maisie clasped her hands to her chest. "I'm so glad you're going to make the most of this beautiful day. A picnic with Kurt sounds perfect."

"That's what I thought," Clara said. "It's supposed to rain for the next eight days. After last week, I hate to even think of it."

"Rough week?" Josef asked.

"I'll say," Clara said. "We barely broke even. If yesterday hadn't been busy, we'd have been in the red for the week."

Josef's brows shot up, and he turned to his wife.

Maisie cleared her throat.

Clara glanced at her business partner, then turned her attention back to Josef. "I'm sorry. Didn't you know?"

"I looked at the receipts, as usual," Maisie replied instead, running her hands down the front of her robe. "The diner had a slow week, too. Nothing unexpected or out of the ordinary."

"If you'd have told me, I could have helped." Josef squared his shoulders.

Clara looked at the kind older man who she regarded as a wise father figure.

"I've been meaning to talk to you." He glanced at his wife, who was giving him an icy stare. He ignored it and continued. "I think you should limit the items you offer at Sweets & Treats. You aren't making money on all of them. Figure out which ones are profitable and ditch the rest."

Clara took a half-step back. The butterflies in her stomach that the church service had vanquished came swooping back.

"I know a thing or two about the restaurant business," he continued, warming to his topic.

"Of course you do," Clara replied.

"Take cupcakes, for example. I researched online and learned that those are a bakery's most profitable item."

"I'm aware of that. We offer a variety of cupcakes, including a flavor of the week." Clara felt her cheeks flush.

"Those macarons. They're fabulous, but so time-consuming to make. Are you charging enough?"

"I am. The macarons are one of our best money makers." Her reply sounded curt even to her own ears.

Maisie put her hand on her husband's elbow. "We don't need to have an impromptu business meeting right now."

"I'm only trying to help." Josef looked at the two women he loved. "I understand how challenging it is to start a business, let alone one dealing with food. And I know that you're working way too hard, Clara." He rubbed his hands together. "I've lived with the stress of this business and it's awful. I want things to be easy for you."

Clara forced a smile. "I know you do, Josef. You have a depth of expertise and I'm grateful that you share it with me."

The creases in his forehead eased. "I'm here for you. Call me anytime."

"I know," Clara said. "And I will. Soon. I promise."

"I also want to say"—Maisie looked pointedly at her husband —"that while we have some experience with running a bakery, we've never run a patisserie. You have expertise, Clara, that we don't have. You're smart, knowledgeable, and savvy. That—and the fact that you're the best baker I've ever met—are why I went into business with you."

Clara's smile brightened.

"Take our advice into consideration but make your own decisions." She gave Josef a side eye. "I have confidence in you."

"Thank you," Clara said, leaning in to hug Maisie. "That means the world to me."

"We both do," Josef said, and a parishioner pulled him away.

Maisie held Clara at arm's length and looked directly into her eyes. "Ignore Josef and that lawyer boyfriend of yours," she said.

Clara drew back in surprise.

"I've been getting an earful from both of them about my cooking school plans," Maisie said.

Clara nodded. "Everyone's quick to offer advice."

"Exactly. Whether solicited or not. Frankly, I've had it up to here"—she motioned to her throat—"with both of them."

"Sounds like we need to talk," Clara said.

"I'd like that. We're both pursuing dreams and don't need people planting seeds of doubt."

"We do enough of that on our own," Clara agreed. "I'll be at Sweet & Treats the entire week. If it's raining, we won't be busy. Stop by anytime. We'll circle the wagons to help each other."

Maisie's eyes held their customary twinkle. "I love the sound of that. I'll see you tomorrow."

Clara gave her a thumbs-up.

"Now—get out of here. Have a wonderful day with Kurt. And don't think about our bakery."

Clara grinned, and they each stepped away, buoyed by the support they felt from the other.

CHAPTER 8

urt tucked the manilla envelope under his arm. "It's still muddy, so watch your step." He took her hand and led her around the worst of the slippery patches to the front of the house.

"I want you to see it as if you were entering the house for the first time."

"Should I turn around while you unlock the door?"

"Good idea," Kurt said, inserting his key in the lock as she put her back to him. He pushed the door open wide, then turned to her. "Okay. Ready."

Clara spun around. The morning sun slanted through windows on either side of the open doorway, casting elongated shadows across the warm hardwood floor inside. Freshly painted walls replaced the stained and peeling wallpaper that had been in place the last time she had visited. Baseboards painted a clean off-white created a crisp contrast with the floors.

Kurt extended his arm, inviting her to enter.

"Wow. What a difference refinishing the floors and painting the ceilings and walls has made."

"Right? It doesn't look sad and dilapidated anymore."

"Not in the least."

He led her to the stairs. "Turns out, they only needed refinishing, too."

They climbed to the second floor and examined the two bedrooms.

"Expanding the bathroom and giving the main bedroom a decent closet is worth giving up the third bedroom," he said. He cut his eyes to her. "If I ever need more bedrooms—for kids—I'll add on to the back of the house."

Clara busied herself examining the stack of tile in the upstairs bath. She didn't respond to his mention of children. "This will be gorgeous. You'll be happy you spent the extra money on upgraded tile." She looked from the two boxes on the floor to the interior of the expanded room. "Will this be enough tile?"

"There's a lot more stacked in the kitchen. I hauled it out here yesterday and brought it into the house. The installers come in the morning. I'll let them carry it upstairs."

"Good thinking. How's the half bath you added downstairs?"

"Come see for yourself." He led the way downstairs and around the corner.

"It's fabulous! Is this the tile you put down yesterday?"

He nodded.

"You did a beautiful job. If this lawyer thing doesn't work out, you've got a future as a tile installer."

Kurt rubbed his still-sore lower back. "I think I'll stick with practicing law."

"I don't blame you." Clara turned toward the kitchen area behind her. "Are the layouts in that envelope you're carrying?"

He shook his head and crossed to a folding table shoved against an outside wall. "The three renditions are here."

She walked to the table and studied each one.

"What do you think?" Kurt asked.

"They're each a functional design. It depends on how you want to use your kitchen."

"What do you mean?"

"How much cooking do you do? Will you entertain? Do you need robust food preparation space? How about seating twelve around a dinner table?"

Kurt bit his lip and shrugged.

"You don't cook much in town, but you don't have time to, either. Out here, it might be different. Food delivery this far into the country is going to be limited, too. You might be forced to cook, but even if you'll be cooking, that doesn't mean you need a large kitchen." She looked at him. "Would you rather have a small basic kitchen and use the rest of the space for a family room?"

"My living room will be casual. I don't need a separate family room." He ran his eyes over her. "I like the idea of a nice big kitchen. One where there's room for two people to cook together. I'm not sure I know twelve people I'd invite to dinner, but I love the idea."

"Then I can tell you which design is the clear winner for that vision of this house." She picked up the design that showed floor-to-ceiling cabinets with countertops on three walls, had a large central island with an extra sink, two dishwashers, double ovens, and a built-in microwave. "I'll bet this one is double the cost of the others," she said. "The extra cabinets and countertops alone will be a small fortune."

"It is, but I plan to keep this place for the rest of my life. I want it to fit my lifestyle now and in the future."

Their eyes met, and she smiled. "This is the one I would want, too."

He took the drawing from her and rolled it, securing it with a rubber band. "I'll call the designer first thing tomorrow so she can order everything. With luck, it'll be installed before the holidays."

"What's in that envelope you've been clutching since we got out of your truck?"

"Old photos my grandmother saved that I found yesterday. I

thought it would be fun to show them to you while we were here —in the spot where they were taken."

Clara clasped her hands together. "I love that!"

"Let's set up our picnic on the front porch," Kurt said. "We'll go through them while we eat."

"Can we sit on the steps? I need to drink in as much sunshine and nice weather as possible."

Kurt nodded in agreement and walked out to his truck to retrieve the sandwiches, chips, pickles, and sodas he'd purchased from the Pinewood General Store on the way to pick her up. "I didn't get us cookies," he said. "After Sweets & Treats cookies, nothing else will do."

"Wise man," Clara responded. "For the record, I won't be mad if you eat pastries made by someone else."

"You won't think I'm cheating on you?" he teased.

"Nope. Don't tell anyone, but I occasionally eat an Oreo or two myself."

He feigned surprise. "Your secret is safe with me."

They spread the food on top of painter's plastic laid out on the porch. Clara scooted next to Kurt, and they worked their way through the photos as they nibbled at their lunch.

"I love the Christmas ones," Clara said. "Actually, I love all of them, but it's fun to think about where you'll put your Christmas tree. It looks good here"—she tapped a photo—"by the fireplace, but I think it would be spectacular if you moved it to the corner on the other side of the room. That way, you'd see it from the living room and the kitchen."

"I hadn't thought about a tree yet." He held up the last photo. "Guess who that incredibly handsome toddler is."

"You—of course. It looks just like you. You're a bit taller now than you were back then"—a smile flashed across her lips—"but the face is all you."

She took the photo and studied it for a long time. "Your parents?"

"He nodded."

"You look like a very happy family."

"We were."

"Was that where they hung the swing?" she asked, turning and pointing to the eyebolts in the ceiling of the porch.

"Yep. Too bad I don't still have that swing."

"You could get another one."

"I've been looking. Everything I've found is a cheap imitation of the one that my grandfather made." He told her his memories of the swing.

Clara listened with rapt attention. By the time he mentioned "pirate ship," she'd decided she'd find some way to replace that handmade wooden swing for the man she had fallen in love with.

CHAPTER 9

$\mathcal{C}$lara stood at the window of Sweets & Treats. The display was full of colorful macarons arranged in an arching rainbow. Sugar cookies iced to look like smiley faces appeared to be grinning at loaves of artisan bread. A tray of the cupcake flavor of the week—peaches and cream—filled a tiered stand.

The tableau inside the glass didn't mirror the scene on the other side. Rain came down in sheets, a stiff breeze blowing it against the glass.

Joan came up behind Clara. "It's a stunning window display."

Clara nodded without turning around. "Too bad no one is going to see it."

"You don't know that," Joan said. "It's only mid morning. Maybe we'll be busy during lunch."

Clara held out her phone to her bakery supervisor. The weather app on the screen called for steady rain and increasing winds for the rest of the day.

"I know," Joan said. "I saw that." She sucked in a breath. "I've got an idea for you."

"Okayyy." Clara drew the word out.

"We don't need to bake anything else today. We've got more than enough inventory on hand."

Clara closed her eyes and nodded. "I agree. Send the bakers home. With pay—make sure they know I won't dock their wages."

"You can't keep paying people for work they're not doing," Joan said. "We thought—"

"No." Clara interrupted her. "I've got the best crew of bakers I've ever encountered. They care about our products. Everyone who works here needs the money—and I'm sure some turned down other jobs that offer more security." Her shoulders straightened as she gained steam. "I won't make them suffer because we're not busy. It's my job as the owner of this patisserie to manage cash flow."

"I agree with every word," Joan said. "That's why I came to work for you." She cleared her throat. "The idea I want to discuss with you came from Susan, by the way." She gestured with her head to the workroom. "They know we'll be forced to give away most of what we baked today. That worries them, too. They may not be owners, but they're invested emotionally in our success, you know."

"I'm aware. Having that support from our staff means the world to me." Clara closed her eyes as she inhaled slowly. "It also makes me aware that it's not only my future—my hopes and dreams—that are at stake here. Anyway—what's her idea?"

"She'd like to set up a social media account for the bakery. Two of the women follow patisseries in Paris and they showed me their posts. I couldn't stop watching. It's so interesting."

"I probably follow the same ones," Clara said.

"I had them set up my account, so I'll see them from now on. One of these French bakers has almost a million followers. Can you believe it?"

A smile cracked through Clara's stern expression. "I can. Be careful," she warned. "Once you get started scrolling through posts, it's impossible to stop. You'll look up and hours will have gone by."

"Which is exactly why Sweets & Treats needs its own account."

"It's on my list—my extremely long list—of things to do."

"That's why I brought it up. Susan and the other bakers want to handle it for you. Managing social media won't be another thing added to your already too busy schedule."

"It's not as simple as creating an account," Clara said. "Businesses need to have a consistent look and message."

"Branding. Your platform needs to reflect the feel of your business."

Clara's brows shot up like toast from a toaster.

"Susan's working on a marketing degree online." Joan talked faster as she warmed to her subject. "You've got a talented bunch back there."

"I guess I do."

"Your color palette needs to match the shop." She pointed to the cheery pastel shades of pink, green, blue, and yellow around them. "This reminds her of the set of that British baking show. She says it's brilliant."

"What else has Susan said?"

"Our brand is the highest quality, with a nod to luxury. We provide staples, and we're also continuously experimenting to bring our customers the latest in French patisserie."

"Gosh," Clara said, straightening her shoulders, "that makes me feel—I don't know—very grand."

"You *are* grand. Susan says your messaging needs to reflect that. She's created a spreadsheet with a content creation and posting schedule."

"Holy cow! That's incredible."

"Betty is good at taking videos on her phone. Even her grandkids call her the family photographer. We'd post videos of you in the workroom and the storefront. You could explain how a patisserie operates, give baking or entertaining tips, or just be having fun with customers."

"Sounds like I'll need to spend more time on my hair and makeup in the morning, so I'm camera-ready."

"No. You need to look natural." Joan smiled at her boss. "Besides, you're young and beautiful. You don't need to worry."

"Did Susan come up with all this today?"

Joan shook her head. "She didn't tell any of us, but she's been working on it at home in the evenings for weeks."

"That's incredibly kind of her."

"So—you'll do it? We think it'll help get the word out about Sweets & Treats."

Clara felt a lump rising in her throat. "You bet I will. Let's start now?"

"That's what we're hoping you'd say." Joan turned toward the workroom. "Everyone's got a part to play in this—whether it's setting up a shot, writing an outline of a video post, or coming up with hashtags. We're all in."

Clara swallowed the emotion rising inside her. Ten minutes ago, she'd been staring at the rain, feeling sorry for herself. Now, she knew she was the luckiest patisserie owner in the world. "I can't wait to see Susan's plans. Lead the way."

CHAPTER 10

"Steam is crucial to baking bread." Clara stood in front of the open door of the commercial steam oven and focused on Betty's phone. "It keeps the crust moist so that the dough can expand and stretch before the crust sets. You'll get a lighter crumb texture that way. Here's a tip if you don't have one of these," she gestured to the computerized electronic panel of her oven that was the size of a refrigerator. "Line an enameled cast iron Dutch oven with parchment paper. Add your dough, slip an ice cube between the pan and the parchment, and bake with the lid firmly in place." Clara had almost completed the third take of her explanation when a series of urgent knocks sounded on the rear entrance into the patisserie.

Joan raced to the door and opened it.

Maisie stood on the other side, struggling with an umbrella on the verge of being turned inside out and blowing away in the wind.

Joan pulled her former boss into the workroom and closed the door. "Gracious," she said. "What are you doing out on an afternoon like this?"

Maisie shut her umbrella and stood it against the wall. "I was wondering that myself." She brushed water from the sleeves of her raincoat before taking it off and hanging it on a hook by the door. "I wanted to talk to Clara and—based on the forecast—I'd be traipsing around in the pouring rain no matter when I came here."

She hugged Joan and went around the room, hugging and greeting the other bakers. They'd all worked for Maisie when she'd run the bakery operation behind the diner. Her stroke had forced her to step back from the bakery and, at the urging of her over-protective husband and Kurt, she'd sold the bakery equipment to Clara.

The two women had gone into partnership to form Sweets & Treats. Maisie was satisfied she had made the right decision by closing her bakery operation, but once fully recovered from her stroke, she had been bored and restless.

The idea of starting a cooking school had dawned on her several months earlier, and she'd known instantly that it was what she wanted to do. Maisie had always wanted to be a teacher. She was confident she could pass on her passion for cooking to students of all ages. The name of her school—*Good Food - Great Life*—reflected her belief that a good meal helped people live a great life.

"What am I interrupting?" She looked from the stacks of baked artisan breads on a worktable to Betty, holding her cell phone, to Clara wearing a crisp white apron and a fresh coat of lipstick.

"We were recording a reel," Joan said.

All faces turned to Maisie with an expectant air.

"I know what a reel is," she said, a sliver of indignation in her voice. "We use it at the diner. I'm not that out of it, you know."

"Of course you're not," Clara said, coming to her side and putting an arm around her shoulders. "Do we need to do another take?" She looked at Betty and Susan.

Susan shook her head. "We filmed enough today to get us started. Betty and I will work on this tonight."

"Leave it until tomorrow afternoon," Clara said. "If it's anything like today, you'll have plenty of time on your hands. I want to see and approve everything before you post it."

"That works," Susan said. "We'll need your input to set up the account, too."

"It's closing time," Joan said. "I'll bring in the sign and lock up."

"We'll clean out the cases before we leave," one baker said.

"Clara and I will do that while we talk," Maisie said. "Unless you want to take something home to your families, you can go."

Goodbyes were said, and Maisie and Clara were soon alone in the workroom. The compressors of the refrigerators and freezers hummed. Rain pounded on the roof.

Clara and Maisie entered the front of the shop and began boxing the unsold pastries.

"Someone will be happy to receive these," Maisie said.

"I thought I'd drop them at the fire station," Clara said. "I spread our excess product around to different businesses."

"That's kind," Maisie replied.

"Not entirely." Clara looked at Maisie. "I hope someone new will sample our stuff and decide to place an order. I'm not that selfless."

"There's nothing wrong with trying to be successful," Maisie retorted.

"Anyway—you came by to talk about your cooking class?"

"Yes. I'm starting with a series of ten two-hour classes. I'll teach a basic technique or skill at each lesson and have the students use it to prepare a meal to take home. I'll have three breakfasts, three lunches, three dinners, and a final session devoted to stocking a pantry, learning to have ingredients on hand to turn out a delicious meal at a moment's notice."

"I need to audit that last lesson." Clara smiled at the older woman. "That sounds like a helpful way to organize things."

Maisie nodded. "I'll include basic knife skills, sauteing, roasting, and frying. We'll learn about leavening agents, thickening sauces, how to use spices—especially salt—and when it's essential to use fresh ingredients rather than frozen. My students will understand how to make substitutions."

"Hearing you talk, I'm reminded of how much there is to learn to be an accomplished cook."

"There is, but anyone can do it. I want my students to gain the skills my mother and grandmother taught me, so they're confident when they walk into the kitchen. Cooking should be creative and relaxing—not a stressful ordeal spent racing around the kitchen like a pinball shot out of the machine at the beginning of a game."

Clara laughed out loud. "That's an apt analogy. I've done that before."

"Every student will leave the class with a fully cooked meal for a family of four."

"Sign me up! That sounds fabulous. You've thought this through." She placed the last pastry in her box and set it on the counter next to the other ten boxes loaded with the unsold inventory. "I have nothing to add." She studied Maisie. "You know your plan is terrific. Why are you here?"

Maisie released a heavy sigh. "Josef and Kurt think it's too much for me. They want me to cut back or hire someone else to teach with me." She shook her head. "I've spent weeks coming up with this curriculum and it's what I want to teach. Only eight people have signed up. How hard can that be?"

Clara bit her lip.

"What? You think they're right? I'm not a decrepit old lady, you know," Maisie sputtered.

"Of course you aren't." Clara was quick to reassure her. "It's just that you've outlined a very ambitious course. You'll need a lot of one-on-one time with your students, even if there's only eight of them. Do you want my honest opinion?"

Maisie nodded.

"Get some help. The lessons are in the late afternoon, right?"

Maisie nodded again.

"I'm sure one of our bakers will be happy to assist. They're not getting any overtime here. I'd offer to lend a hand, but I'm up to my eyeballs as it is."

"I've heard that you're working non-stop," Maisie said.

"From Kurt?"

"Yes."

"Is he complaining?"

"No. He's worried about you. He and Josef both are."

Clara let her annoyance show. "Which is why they're offering all sorts of suggestions, like closing on Monday in addition to Sunday or cutting back on our menu."

"I agree that we shouldn't implement any of those. You know what you're doing, Clara. Follow your instincts."

"You know your stuff, too, Maisie. Keep your course the way it is and hire one of our bakers."

Maisie nodded. "That advice applies to you, too. Asking for and accepting help would be a good idea for you." She fixed her gaze on Clara. "I'm a part owner and you never ask me to do anything."

"You've been busy starting a cooking school, for heaven's sake. Besides—I'm getting help. Susan and Betty have taken the reins on setting up a social media presence for Sweets & Treats."

"And I heard you tell them you want to see and approve everything they do. You don't get high marks for delegation that way."

Clara turned to the counter and swept away an imaginary crumb. "Point taken. I'll only do that until I'm satisfied they've captured the tone I want to set with our account."

"I'm going to hold you to that."

"Please do." Clara nodded. "We both bristle at advice from Kurt and Josef—no matter how well-meaning. But we know we support each other's dreams. Let's make a pact that we'll listen to each other—even if it's something we don't want to hear."

Maisie crooked her little finger and held it out to Clara. "Pinky swear?"

Clara hooked her pinky into Maisie's. "Pinky swear."

CHAPTER 11

Clara tucked her laptop under her arm and churned through her purse with one hand to retrieve her ringing cell phone while juggling her keys with the other. She tapped at the screen and brought it to her ear. "Hi, Kurt."

"Hi, sweetheart. You sound out of breath."

She hesitated before she answered. He was supposed to pick her up in five minutes for their regular Wednesday night dinner date. "I got home later than I'd planned, so I'm racing around getting ready." She looked at her locked front door ten paces in front of her and felt bad about her little white lie. She'd canceled on him the prior two Wednesdays and didn't want to admit that she'd be late tonight.

He was probably calling to tell her he'd be late, and she'd have time to change out of her baker's uniform of black slacks, sensible black shoes, and white shirt into a pretty summer dress. Kurt was important to her, and she wanted him to feel that she made an effort with her appearance—even on days when she had been on her feet twelve straight hours and wanted nothing more than to collapse into her claw-footed tub for a steaming bubble bath.

"I hate to do this at the last minute, but I need to cancel. My mediation hearing is still going and—all of a sudden—we're making progress. I think we've got a real shot at settling this case if we stay at it."

"Then, by all means, that's what you should do. I know how much time you spent preparing for today. I'm glad it's working out." The drizzle that had accompanied her on the drive home had turned into a steady rain. She tried to insert her key into the lock without making noise but abandoned her efforts when the laptop threatened to slip out of its perch on her hip. She pressed herself into the door to take advantage of the slim protection provided by the arched pediment above it.

"I'm really sorry to leave you in the lurch for dinner," he continued, his tone conveying his sincerity.

"Don't worry about that. I've got plenty of stuff in my refrigerator." Another white lie, she thought, knowing that she'd heat a can of soup and call it good.

"I've got to go. Talk tomorrow."

"Good luck," Clara said. "Love you."

They ended the call. She dropped her phone back into her purse, hitched up the laptop that seemed determined to escape, and unlocked her door.

Noelle wasn't waiting to greet her.

Clara dropped her things on the entry table and raced to the kitchen. The back door was closed, and she breathed a sigh of relief.

She couldn't handle Noelle getting lost again, like she had during last winter's blizzard. Her pup had gotten into her back garden and had dug herself out under the fence. Ian had followed her and they had become lost in the dangerous storm. Ian's quick wittedness had led them to shelter in a nearby preschool, saving both their lives.

Clara knew where she'd find her sweet dog. Noelle had wormed her way into the hearts of Ian's family. Even Tabitha had warmed to the small pup with the big personality and constantly wagging tail. Noelle would be firmly ensconced at the big house.

The rain was now coming down in sheets. Clara thought about grabbing an umbrella but opted for her waterproof poncho instead. Noelle despised getting her paws wet. She'd have to carry her girl from the big house to her guest cottage.

Clara hurried along the path to the larger home at the front of the property, her head bent against the wind as she pulled the poncho forward to shield herself from the rain.

The rear door opened as she climbed the steps from the backyard.

"I saw you coming," Laura Ramsey said. "It's not a decent night for man nor beast."

"Thanks," Clara said, dashing inside. "Is Noelle here?"

"She is." Laura closed the door against the storm. "We're in the kitchen. Ian just got home from his cooking class. He thought you were going out with Kurt tonight. Ian knows how scared Noelle is of thunder and lightning, so he brought her here to spend the evening with us. He said he left you a note."

"I only got home a moment ago," Clara said, water running off her poncho onto the mat. "I didn't see a note."

Laura looked at her blankly. "Can Noelle stay with us while you're out?"

"Kurt had to cancel, so I'm home for the evening."

"I'm sorry to hear that."

Clara's mouth twisted into a wry smile. "I don't mind. I've got a ton of work to do tonight."

"You're always busy," Laura remarked. Her head came up, and she clasped her hands together. "Stay for supper."

"I'm here to get Noelle," Clara said. "You don't need to bother—"

"It's no trouble. Ian brought home chicken piccata from tonight's class. He's so proud of the meals he's fixing. I'm positive he'd love to show you."

Clara sniffed the air.

"Smells wonderful, doesn't it?"

"It sure does. Do you have enough? Ian's a growing boy—I'll bet he can eat two servings."

"I think Maisie has taken that into account when she distributes ingredients to the students. I know they're supposed to take home a meal that feeds four, but I've never seen a family of four eat the mountain of food Ian brings home. He has enough for lunch the next day."

Clara chuckled. "That sounds like Maisie."

Ian poked his head into the doorway from the kitchen. "Dinner's ready," he said, a smile slashing across his face when he saw Clara. "Hi! Aren't you going out with Kurt?"

Clara shook her head no.

"Can you stay for dinner? Maisie told me I did really well—that she couldn't have made better chicken piccata herself." Pride was stamped on his features.

"I'd love to," Clara said. She followed him into the kitchen. Tabitha sat at the farmhouse table, stroking Harry, the cat that practically lived on her lap. Ron and Hermione, his siblings, were intertwined in their bed in the corner.

Noelle was stretched out under Tabitha's chair. She wagged her tail at the sight of her mistress but remained in her cozy spot. Tabitha fished a treat out of her pocket and lowered her hand to Noelle. The little dog accepted the offering without getting up.

Clara shook her head but said nothing. Noelle had made a dog-loving convert out of Tabitha, and she wouldn't interfere with that.

"Your mom and I were remarking about how good this smells. Need help with anything?"

"Nope. Take a seat and I'll bring it to the table. Maisie says serving family style is the best."

"I agree." Clara slid into a chair next to Tabitha.

Ian brought a bowl of egg noodles, a dish of roasted broccoli, and the platter of fragrant chicken piccata to the table.

Tabitha poured Clara a glass of water and passed it to her. "Hello, dear," she said. "Nice to see you. This is my only contribution to meals these days. I serve water." She chuckled. "After being so sick this winter, I'm glad to be able to do that."

Laura said grace, and they tucked into the delicious meal.

Clara took several bites, then dabbed her lips with her napkin. "This is perfect, Ian. The chicken is moist and juicy. That's difficult to do with white meat—it dries out fast. The sauce is the right balance of salty and lemony. Well done."

Ian's smile bloomed again.

"Are you enjoying the classes?"

"They're great!"

"How about the other students?"

"One older guy dropped out. He said he didn't want to learn to cook after all. It's easier for him to eat out."

"That's disappointing."

"Maisie told me it's okay. She said he's a recent widower and the thought of cooking in his kitchen might be too much for him right now."

"Maisie is one of the kindest and most intuitive persons I've ever known," Tabitha commented.

"Is Betty helping?"

"Yep. She's great. You should see how fast she whips around the kitchen. Maisie gets impatient with her at times."

"Oh?" Clara paused with her fork halfway to her mouth.

"Maisie keeps saying she can do things. She doesn't need so much help."

"Does Maisie look tired or anything? Teaching the class isn't too much for her?" Clara wasn't sure that a boy entering the seventh grade would be the best judge of this.

Ian rested his fork on his plate. "I've been watching her. Great grandma told me to." He looked at the old woman, who nodded in acknowledgement. "I think she's doing fine."

Clara lifted questioning eyes to Tabitha.

"I've been friends with Maisie since before any of you were born," Tabitha said. "She and I talk. I know everyone is worried she's going to keel over if she so much as breaks a sweat." Tabitha chuckled. "Us old birds are made of sterner stuff. Still—I thought it would be good if Ian kept an eye on her."

"Thank you," Clara said. "I feel better knowing this. Will you tell me if anything changes—if you think she's overdoing?"

Ian looked at Tabitha. She nodded. "We'll call if we think there's anything to worry about. I'm ready for seconds." Tabitha reached for the platter, skewered another chicken breast, and sent the platter around the table. "What's new with you? We've been following you on that thing." She pointed to her granddaughter's phone on the kitchen island. "Very entertaining."

Clara put a hand to her head. "That's nice to hear. Betty and Susan—two of my bakers—have been extra busy creating content. It's fun, but a lot of work for them and me."

"How are things with that young man of yours?" Tabitha continued.

"They're great. We're both extremely busy with our careers right now, so we don't see each other as much as we'd like."

"Take a piece of advice from an old lady. If you love this man —if you think he might be the one—make sure he knows how you feel about him. Even if you can't spend a lot of time together, make sure he knows you're thinking of him. Find the time to do special things."

"Funny you say that," Clara said. "I've decided on a gift for him."

"It's a long time until Christmas," Laura said.

"I'm not waiting for an occasion to give it."

"A 'just because' gift?" Tabitha grinned. "Those are the best kind."

"It's a wooden porch swing for his new house. He's purchased his grandparent's home outside of town and is renovating it."

"I heard about that," Laura replied. "You knew them, didn't you, Granny?"

Tabitha nodded. "They were a lovely couple. That sounds like an extremely thoughtful gift."

"I've searched everywhere I can think of online and haven't found one that fits the style of the house or is high enough quality. I'm not buying anything with a two-star review."

"You'll need to have it custom-made." Tabitha looked at her granddaughter. "Don't you know someone through your school who's a woodworker?"

"One of the other teachers has a brother who's a firefighter and does woodworking on the side."

"Do you think he could make me a swing?"

"He builds custom furniture all the time. I'll get you his number tomorrow."

"Awesome," Clara said. "That's a huge relief."

"Glad we could help," Laura said, rising to clear the table.

Clara and Ian got up to help.

"I've got this," Laura said, looking at Ian and Clara. "Two hard-and-fast household rules are that the cook doesn't clean up, and guests don't either."

"I agree that Ian shouldn't lift a finger, but I don't consider myself a guest anymore. We're practically family."

"We *do* think of you as family." Laura looked at Clara. "You're going to pull out your laptop and work until midnight once you leave us." It was a statement rather than a question.

Clara shrugged and looked away from Laura's thoughtful gaze.

"I'm going to watch TV and go to bed. That's it. Please let me finish up here so you can go home and get busy. Maybe you'll crawl into bed a bit earlier that way. The idea makes me happy."

The backs of Clara's eyes stung, and she blinked rapidly. She took the plates in her hands and set them on the counter by the sink.

Laura followed her and pointed out the window. "The rain has let up. You'd better take Noelle home while you can still convince her to walk on her own."

Noelle popped up from under the table, as if on cue, and hurried to the door.

Laura and Clara chuckled.

"That settles it," Laura said, walking Clara to the back door.

"Thank you for a lovely dinner," Clara said, pulling on her poncho.

The women hugged. "I'm so grateful to be part of your extended family," Clara whispered in Laura's ear.

"The feeling's mutual." Laura pulled back and opened the door. "Now—go. And don't stay up late. You'll be more effective with a good night's sleep."

Noelle raced down the steps and relieved herself as soon as she hit the grass.

Clara descended the stairs, and they trotted toward home.

CHAPTER 12

$\mathcal{K}$urt stepped into Sweets & Treats, the wind chasing him inside. The bell over the door tinkled in a friendly fashion.

Clara stood on the first rung of her stepladder, a drill in her right hand, a hammer clutched between her knees, and a pair of wall anchors and screws held in her teeth.

Kurt rushed to her side. "I told you last night I'd take care of this."

Clara rested her hips against the ladder and turned her head to him. "And I said I've got this." She mumbled around the hardware in her teeth. She turned back to the wall and drilled holes at both of the spots she'd marked with a pencil.

Kurt reached up to take the drill from her.

Clara inserted the wall anchors in the holes, tapped them into place with the hammer, and added the screws.

"Is this what you want to hang?"

She nodded, and he picked up the bulletin board propped against the baseboard. "I guess you didn't need my help," he remarked. "I thought you weren't good at such tasks." He handed her the board. The frame featured painted cupcakes, cookies, eclairs, and croissants in colors that matched the shop's decor. 'The Bread Board' was lettered in a scroll-y font across the top.

"I watched a video this morning that showed how to do it. Easy-peasy." Clara hung the board on the screws and straightened it. "Does it look level?"

Kurt took several steps back. "Scootch it up a quarter inch on the right."

She made the adjustment.

"Perfect," he said.

Clara stepped off the ladder and joined him, admiring her handiwork.

"That looks great," Kurt said.

"Thanks." She leaned against him. "I'm going to post our weekly specials, and the flyer Maisie made for her fall cooking classes. Nick will put up information about guitar lessons. I'm working on a suggestion box for our customers, and I'll publicize it on the board." She turned her face to his. "It's a community information board. Do you have anything you'd like to post?"

"Let me think about that. I'm sure people at the office would love to take advantage of this. Our receptionist is spearheading a back-to-school backpack drive."

"Tell her she can drop off a flyer—or email it to me and I'll print and post it."

"Will do," Kurt said, fighting the urge to take her in his arms and kiss her. "One suggestion?"

Clara arched an eyebrow.

"I know we've discussed this and I've agreed I won't offer advice," he added hastily, "but you need to think about this. Don't offer to print stuff out for people. You want to increase traffic into your shop, so make them come in to post things. No one can step inside here without buying something. Those cases are amazing."

"That's a terrific suggestion." Clara looped her arm around his shoulders and gave him a quick kiss.

"I thought we weren't doing public displays of affection," he whispered as she drew back.

"No one is in here, so we're not in public."

"Good point," Kurt said, pulling her back to him. "I appreciate a careful adherence to the rules. You should have been a lawyer."

Clara laughed, and they kissed again. "As much as I enjoy snogging you," she said, "I wish the weather would improve so I'd be knee-deep in customers."

"It's supposed to be sunny by midday," he said.

"That's something to look forward to."

"And I need a dozen of…" He looked at the cases. "Everything. To take back to my firm. If they find out I was here and didn't bring in treats, I'll have a riot on my hands."

She touched his cheek. "It's not your responsibility to make Sweets & Treats a success. It's incredibly kind of you, but you don't have to buy out my shop every time you come in."

"My motives are entirely selfish," he retorted. "Everyone works harder when I bring in treats from Sweets & Treats. They're happier and get along better. Productivity soars."

"Could I get a video testimonial to post on social media?" Clara said jokingly and moved to the bakery cases. She folded a pink box into position and began filling it with cherry Danish.

Kurt snagged one of the pastries and took a bite. "They're my favorite. Might as well make sure I get one."

Clara replaced the one he had taken and moved on to chocolate croissants.

Kurt finished his pastry and licked a smear of sweet cherry goo from his fingers. "What I said—about the effect your treats have on my employees—is true. Feeling appreciated is important. An unexpected kindness—even as small as a pastry—lifts spirits. You wait and see—my firm is going to have a very good day. Thanks to you."

Clara looked at him over the case. "That's one of the nicest things anyone's ever said to me. I needed to hear that. My spirits have been low all month."

He held her gaze. "I meant every word, Clara. Sweets & Treats is making Pinewood a better place."

Clara finished boxing his order and rang it up. She took the last cherry Danish from the case, wrapped it in parchment, and placed it in a bag on top of the boxes. "You deserve a second cherry Danish for that. On the house."

"I won't say no to that," he said. "I was already planning to open the box and fish one out when I got to my car."

Clara laughed. "I'll walk you out."

The sun was peeking between the clouds.

"I think you're right—we're going to have at least one nice day this week."

"Let's celebrate with dinner and a movie Saturday night," he replied as he carefully stowed the bakery boxes in his car.

"Wonderful idea. I haven't been to a movie in ages."

"What do you want to see?"

"Surprise me. As long as it's not horror, I'm good." She leaned in and kissed him. "Thank you for bringing sunshine into my world, even on dark days."

CHAPTER 13

Kurt and Clara strolled hand-in-hand on the wide sidewalk to the movie house that remained open for business in downtown Pinewood. The old-fashioned marquee, outlined in large, white light bulbs, announced the name of the movie.

"I thought you would have preferred to see the summer's blockbuster action film in the multiplex by the mall," Clara said. "On a wide screen with surround sound."

"Those are great," he agreed. "But nothing beats the red velvet curtain that opens at the start of the movie or the art déco lobby. Not to mention, their popcorn is still the best. I think they use real butter."

He looked at her as their hands swung and continued, "This feels like more of a date night than joining the throng at the mall theater. It's release weekend and they're predicting sell-out crowds. The multiplex is showing this movie on four screens."

"You're a romantic at heart, Kurt Holbrook. And I completely agree." Clara squeezed his hand. "I'm not in the mood for dealing with crowds."

They walked by the menswear store, now closed after hours,

and Clara pulled them to the door. "Look." She pointed to a bulletin board hung next to the door. "They've put up a board like mine—except theirs is protected from the elements by plexiglass. I'll have to call to tell them it looks fabulous."

"You know the owner?"

"I met him earlier in the week. I went door-to-door, suggesting the downtown merchants put up community bulletin boards." She scanned the posted notices. "Maisie's tacked up her cooking school flyer."

Kurt leaned in to examine it. "She's going full steam, isn't she? There are evening and Saturday classes until the end of the year."

"Good Food - Great Life has taken off, that's for sure. Her first class—the one that Ian took—was a home run. A student posted about it on social media, and it went viral. Her phone's been ringing off the hook ever since."

"That's awesome. She deserves every bit of her success."

"Absolutely. I wish I got the results with my social media that she's had. I'm pressing hard to build my presence there because it works."

Kurt was quiet, scrutinizing Maisie's flyer. "Teaching all this would be a lot for anyone. Is Maisie up to this?"

"She's got plenty of help. Most of my bakers work part-time for her, too. They prep the food for lessons, set up the workstations and clean them afterward, and she has at least two helpers when she's teaching. Maisie is free to do what she does best—help people learn to cook. And she loves it."

"I'm glad to hear it."

"You don't need to worry. I keep an eye on her. Frankly, I wouldn't attempt to run those classes without assistance."

They resumed their stroll.

"Speaking of help"—he glanced at her—"are you still supervising everything that happens at Sweets & Treats?"

"Yes. Of course. It's my business." Clara's arm stiffened. "I employ a dozen bakers. I have help."

"Let me rephrase the question," he said in lawyerly fashion. "Do you continue to have your nose planted firmly in everything that goes on there?"

"Objection! Argumentative."

Kurt laughed. "Sustained. I don't want to stir up trouble—especially on date night." He stopped and faced her. "I worry that you're working yourself into the ground. I see your social media posts. They're so well done. Those take a ton of time."

"Susan and Betty handle them."

"You're not micromanaging them?"

"I'm only making sure they capture my voice," Clara huffed. "My brand has to be accurately represented."

"And visiting the downtown merchants to get this bulletin board thing going?"

"It wasn't much work. Everyone was enthusiastic about participating."

"I'm sure they were, sweetheart. You're doing wonderful things. But just because it's a worthwhile thing to do, doesn't mean you have to be the one to do all of it."

Clara sniffed.

Kurt brought her hand to his lips and kissed it. "When we talk at night, you sound exhausted. I've occasionally wondered if you've fallen asleep while I've been talking."

"No...."

"Not that I'd blame you. I get long-winded on the subjects of sports and the legal system."

"I love hearing about your day and things you care about. I'm interested."

"And I care about you." He checked his watch. "We'd better hustle or we won't have time to load up on popcorn and snacks before the movie starts."

They found their seats as the opening credits rolled. Even without amplified sound, the explosions, sirens, and special effects of the summer blockbuster were deafening.

Halfway through the movie, Kurt leaned over to offer Clara a red vine candy.

Her head rested against her seat at an awkward angle. She was sound asleep.

Kurt put his arm around her shoulders and shook her gently.

She woke with a start.

He took her hand and stood, pulling her up with him and out of the theater.

"What're you doing?" she asked when they reached the lobby.

"I'm taking you home. You were asleep."

"No. I'm enjoying it."

"What's happened so far?"

She looked at him blankly. "I only nodded off for a sec."

He shook his head. "Dead to the world."

Clara's face fell. "I'm so sorry, Kurt."

He shrugged.

"Let's go back in. You were looking forward to this. I'll be fine. If I nod off again, ignore me."

He led them to the sidewalk. "I'll catch it when it's on one of the streaming services."

They walked to his car in silence, and didn't talk during the short drive to her place.

He walked her to her door.

"Do you want to come in?"

He shook his head. "You need to sleep."

"I'm sorry. I spoiled our date."

"I'm no stranger to putting all my attention on my career. I get it."

Noelle stuck her nose through a crack in the curtains and barked.

Clara turned her face to his.

He looked away. "Go take care of your girl," Kurt said. "But I want you to do one thing for me. Think about what we discussed on the way to the movie. You've canceled, rescheduled, or forgotten about plans we've made all summer long." He paused before he continued. "Think about whether you have room in your life right now for anything other than starting your business."

"Kurt!" Clara cried. "Of course—"

He cut her off. "Think about it." He turned and walked to his car without a backward glance.

~

CLARA CLOSED the door behind her and leaned against it, raking her hands through her hair. What had just happened? Was Kurt breaking up with her?

Noelle jumped on Clara's leg.

Clara moved to the back door without acknowledging her.

Noelle raced into the yard and did her business, racing back to Clara as soon as she was done.

Clara mechanically tossed Noelle her bedtime treat, and headed for her bedroom. She shrugged out of her clothes and left them in a pool on the floor.

She trudged into the bathroom and gave her teeth a cursory swipe with her toothbrush. *He chose to leave the movie,* she thought. *People fall asleep in them all the time.*

Clara rummaged under the sink for her makeup remover cloths, only to discover she was out of them. She slammed the cabinet shut and returned to her bedroom. She'd deal with her face in the morning.

Clara got into bed, bringing the sheet up to her chin.

Noelle jumped onto the bed, and Clara pulled her close.

Kurt had been right. She'd fallen asleep when they'd been on their customary phone call at bedtime—more than once. How could she have been so careless with her relationship? Tears spilled down Clara's cheeks.

Noelle licked them away.

"I've made a stupid mistake," Clara whispered into the fur at Noelle's neck. "Kurt's mad at me. And he's right. I need to apologize and make amends."

Noelle squirmed until she was in position to swipe Clara's damp chin with her tongue.

"I'm too tired to think about this now." She nestled into her pillow. "When I wake up, we're going to come up with a plan."

Noelle thumped her tail against the bed.

"And you're going to help me with it. I will not lose Kurt Holbrook."

CHAPTER 14

Clara woke Sunday morning to sunshine streaming through the crack in her chintz curtains.

Noelle stood next to the bed, her front paws digging at the covers next to Clara's face.

Clara opened her eyes, and Noelle emitted a frantic-sounding woof.

Clara checked the time on her bedside clock. It was almost ten. She threw the covers back and flung herself out of bed.

"You must be in distress, girl," she said as she hurried to the back door.

Noelle raced ahead of her.

Clara opened the door and Noelle ran to her spot and took care of business.

Clara stepped onto the small landing, turning her face to the morning sun. Pinewood hadn't had such a glorious start to the day in months. She surveyed the horizon. There wasn't a cloud in the sky. She clapped her hands, summoning Noelle inside. Clara knew what she needed to do.

She filled Noelle's bowl with kibble and refreshed her water bowl. As Noelle inhaled her breakfast, Clara made herself a cup of coffee. She rummaged in her cupboard and found only the heel of a loaf of bread. A perusal of her refrigerator proved unhelpful.

Clara tossed the rock-hard bread in the trash and leaned against the counter, sipping her coffee. "Here's our plan, Noelle."

Noelle stopped lapping up water and eyed her mistress.

"The most important thing I need to do today is apologize to Kurt and reassure him I value our relationship."

Noelle gave her tail a swish.

"The next most important is my meeting at eleven with that woodworker guy about making Kurt a porch swing. I'd like to get that ordered right away."

Clara took a swig of coffee. "Kurt said he planned to work at Bloom Cottage today." She looked at Noelle, who lowered herself into downward dog.

"His cell coverage out there is spotty. Let's surprise him while he's working. He brings nothing to eat with him, so I'm sure he'll be hungry." She pursed her lips, considering her options. "Croque madame," she said. "I have the ham and cheeses I need in the refrigerators at Sweets & Treats. We use those ingredients in our quiches. I'll make the béchamel sauce there, too. I'll bring one of our portable induction burners with me to make the sandwiches. Kurt said he has power in the house."

Noelle wiggled her bum enthusiastically.

"You can come with me. Just don't tell anyone I brought my dog to the bakery with me. The health department will have my head."

Noelle turned earnest eyes on Clara.

Clara drained her coffee cup. "I'll hit the shower and we'll be on our way." She bent to pat her dog, then headed to her bathroom.

CHAPTER 15

Kurt lost his grip on the hammer. It landed on the top of his sneaker before skittering along the floor. He let out a yelp, then turned back to the molding he was attempting to install around the living room window. The pieces didn't fit together correctly because of his incorrect angle cut. No amount of finessing would make it work. He'd have to pull it down and start over. He cursed under his breath. Nothing was going right today.

He walked to the workstation he'd set up on the front porch and picked up his phone to check for messages. There were none. Kurt raked his fingers through his hair. Had he been too harsh—too hasty—with Clara the prior night? He hadn't thought so, at the time. After a night of tossing and turning, replaying in his mind the scene at her door, he wasn't so sure.

He refreshed the screen on his phone. There still wasn't a message from her. Kurt knew he had terrible cell coverage at the property, but not hearing from her unleashed a wave of panic. He'd contact her tonight unless he heard from her first. He *prayed* he'd hear from her first.

Kurt went inside to the strips of unused molding lying along the wall. The living room window was the widest in the house. The remaining strips were short lengths. A quick calculation told him he'd have to piece four sections together to make it work. He didn't want to do that. He planned to own Bloom Cottage until the day he died. The best course of action was to do it right the first time.

He'd have to drive into town to the home improvement store to get additional molding. He grabbed his phone and took his keys out of his pocket. With any luck, his phone would ping with an undelivered message from Clara on the way to the store.

Kurt set out, driving through the dappled sunshine of trees lush with mid-summer foliage. The azure sky ahead of him was cloudless. His rearview mirror, however, showed a dark bank of clouds creeping up from the horizon.

He was on the outskirts of town when his phone pinged. He pulled into the parking lot of an auto body shop, closed for the day, to check his messages. As he noted his two messages, his expression fell like a souffle when the oven door is slammed shut. A local candidate for political office was asking for donations, and Maisie had invited him to dinner. He texted back a thumbs-up and a heart emoji to Maisie and pulled back onto the road.

Kurt had driven less than a mile when a familiar vehicle, parked in the driveway of a two-story home, caught his eye. He slowed, then swung his truck into a U-turn. He had to know. It was Clara's SUV. The small crease in her rear bumper was unmistakable.

No one was on the road behind him, and he reduced his speed to a crawl. A small white and tan dog he recognized as Noelle dashed out of the garage, followed by Clara. A tall, well-built man was on her heels. He had a trim black beard. A shortened tank top displayed muscular arms and six-pack abs.

Kurt tasted shock, chased by panic.

The man bent over, and gave Noelle a rubdown like they were old friends. When he stood, Clara hugged him.

Kurt put his foot on the gas. He'd seen enough. Now he knew why she was always so tired. It wasn't her commitment to Sweets & Treats.

It had been years since a girlfriend had cheated on him. From the start, Rachel had been committed to him, and he had felt the same way. He'd thought he'd had the same luck with Clara. *What a fool,* he thought.

He turned his truck around again and resumed his errand to buy molding. He'd be happy at Bloom Cottage and make memories there without Clara.

Kurt wished his brave thoughts would vanquish the sick feeling in the pit of his stomach.

CHAPTER 16

*C*lara pulled into her parking spot behind Sweets & Treats. She opened the rear door to allow Noelle to hop onto the pavement.

"That was fun, wasn't it?"

Noelle looked up and wagged her tail.

"He's going to make the perfect swing for Kurt. I'm glad I snuck a picture of that old photo the last time I was at the cottage. That guy said it'll look exactly like the photo. And last a lifetime." She unlocked the door and shooed Noelle inside.

"You need to stay right here," she said, pointing to the doormat. "Noelle. Sit."

The dog obeyed.

Clara held up her hand. "Down. Stay." Clara watched her comply with the commands. "That's a good girl. It'll take me twenty minutes to whip up the sauce. I'll gather everything else we'll need while it's simmering."

She placed a pan on a portable burner and melted butter, whisking in flour and cooking it until the mixture was golden brown. She added a generous amount of milk and whisked until the roux thickened the milk. Clara then reduced the heat and allowed the mixture to simmer, stirring whenever she passed by the burner.

While it cooked, she ferried another portable burner, eggs, ham, a loaf of her favorite sourdough bread, and gruyere and parmesan cheeses to her car. She found one leftover cherry Danish in the refrigerator and placed it in a bakery bag.

Clara checked the time on her phone before dropping it back into her purse. It was now almost two o'clock. She flew back to her sauce and tasted it. The flour was soft and no longer felt gritty on her tongue. She seasoned it with salt.

"Now," she said to Noelle, who watched her from the mat, "time for the secret ingredient." Clara searched through a long row of glass jars on a shelf until she found what she was looking for. "Nutmeg." She pulled a grater out of a drawer and grated the pungent seasoning into the sauce.

She tasted it again. "Perfect."

Clara turned off the burner and poured the hot sauce into a glass container. She screwed on the lid and wrapped it in a towel.

"Ready to go see Kurt?" she asked Noelle, emphasizing the last word.

The pup jumped to her feet.

Clara was placing her purse on her shoulder when a thought hit her. "We'll need something better than water to drink." She headed to the beverage cooler at the front of the shop and selected four cans of the juice-infused sparkling water flavor that she knew Kurt favored. A loud thwack made Clara stop in her tracks as she returned to the workroom.

She deposited the drinks on the counter and dropped her purse to the floor. Crossing to the front window, she saw her Sweets & Treats sign dangling at a precarious angle. A powerful gust of wind sent it careening again.

Clara noticed the solid wall of roiling black clouds headed their way.

She loved that sign. It had been the first thing she'd bought when she'd realized her dream of opening her patisserie. The dream that her mother had encouraged—and funded—on her deathbed.

Kurt had arranged for it to be hung above the shop as a surprise for her. Clara closed her eyes and remembered the first time she'd seen it, hanging over her shop. Happiness washed over her as she savored the memory.

She would not allow a stupid storm to blow down her sign. The weather had destroyed her profits the past few weeks, but it wasn't going to take her sign.

Clara opened the front door and looked up at the sign. One screw had pulled loose, and dangled from the edge of the sign. She'd climb up on her ladder and use her drill to put the screw back into place. That might not be a permanent solution, but with any luck, it would hold until Kurt's maintenance worker could fix it.

"I'll just be another minute, girl," Clara called to Noelle.

She retrieved her ladder and drill and stepped onto the sidewalk. Holding the sign with her left hand while she re-inserted the screw in its anchor with her right proved to be difficult in the intermittent wind gusts. She finally had it properly aligned and employed her drill.

The screw turned. Clara thought she'd been successful until the strongest gust of the afternoon came through. It ripped both anchors from the brick storefront, sending the sign crashing into her. She fell backward, the ladder and sign following her. The wind carried away her scream.

Clara landed on the sidewalk, a loud crack sounding above the wind. The ladder and sign landed on top of her. Her right foot was free, but her left was tangled at an unnatural angle in the rungs of the ladder.

Clara lay back on the pavement, dazed.

Noelle ran out the front door as the wind blew it shut behind her. She raced to her mistress and rested her nose gently on Clara's chin.

Clara took a large gulp of air, followed by a series of steadying breaths.

"I'm okay, girl." She blinked several times. Her vision was clear. "The fall knocked the wind out of me." She wriggled her toes and fingers. Her right arm was fine, but moving her left was unbearably painful. She pushed the sign off of her.

The ankle tangled in the ladder throbbed.

Noelle sat next to her, whimpering.

"We're going to be all right, girl. The front door is locked, so we need to walk around the building to the back door." She rolled to her right and moaned in pain. Clara gritted her teeth and pulled her left foot free of the ladder. Pain shot through her, and she swallowed against a wave of nausea.

She scooted herself into a sitting position, clasping her left arm against her body with her right. She looked at her left leg, the foot still twisted unnaturally.

"I've messed up my ankle and I think I've broken my arm or shoulder or something." Her voice telegraphed her rising panic. "I need help and my phone's inside. I can't get myself to the back door. It's Sunday afternoon and nobody's open."

Clara looked up and down the street, searching for a car—or a pedestrian—anyone she could hail for help. The area was deserted.

Clara fought back tears. "At least it's not the dead of winter. We're safe here until help comes. Even if that isn't until the morning. We won't come to any harm if we have to spend the night."

The wind picked up again, bringing with it a barrage of raindrops that stung like bee stings.

Clara rocked forward, holding her arm, and called Noelle to her, positioning the dog behind her to shelter her from the rain.

Clara and Noelle stayed in this position until an early dusk descended—and the tornado warning sirens blared their ominous message.

CHAPTER 17

Kurt took the stairs at Bloom Cottage two at a time. He double-checked that the upstairs windows were closed and locked. He'd finished installing window molding along the front of the house and had been shocked when he'd loaded his tools in his truck parked in back. The dark clouds he'd noticed on the horizon an hour ago from windows on the back side of the house were bearing down on the tree line.

Satisfied that the upstairs was secure, he locked the front door and exited out the back. The driveway had been paved earlier in the month and was passable, but a storm would flood several low spots on the road back to town. Kurt didn't want to get stranded.

He raced ahead of the storm and was turning onto his street when his phone announced an incoming call from Maisie. He pressed the button on the steering wheel and answered it.

"Hi Kurt. Are you home?"

"Just pulling into my driveway."

"Good. We've had the television on all day. The national weather service has issued a tornado watch."

"I'm not surprised. It looks ominous out there. I was working at Bloom Cottage and decided to get out of there."

"Good thinking," Maisie replied. "Is Clara with you?"

"No."

"Huh. I've been trying to reach her, but she's not answering her phone."

"I haven't seen her since last night." Kurt bit his lip, knowing that statement wasn't true. He didn't want to share what he'd seen with Maisie.

"I'm worried about her," Maisie continued. "I called Laura, and she said Clara's car isn't there, so I know she's not home."

"Clara's probably at Sweets & Treats."

"That's what I thought. My phone app tells me the alarm isn't set."

"There you go. She's at work."

"I also got a notification that our refrigeration equipment at the patisserie is down."

"The circuit breakers must have tripped."

"The lights flickered a couple of times—that sometimes trips them."

"Clara will reset the circuit breakers."

"That's what I thought, but it's been twenty minutes and they're still off."

"Maybe she doesn't know how to flip the breakers?"

"No—she knows. She showed me how to do it last week." She sighed. "I'd run down there myself, but Josef's taken the car to the diner. This is the first time since we became a one-car family that I wish we hadn't."

"Even if you had access to a car, I wouldn't want you going out right now." His automatic windshield wipers engaged as the rain began to fall. "I'll drive over and make sure your refrigerators and freezers are working."

"Thank you, dear. Sweets & Treats has had a tough couple of weeks. We don't need to compound our problems with food spoilage."

"I'm on my way. What's Josef doing at the diner? I thought you made a pact to take Sundays off."

"The reports about the storm were alarming. We decided to close early and send the staff home. Some of them have long drives into the country and we didn't want them out in dangerous weather. I wanted to go with him, but he wouldn't hear of it."

"I agree with him," Kurt said. "Do you want me to come stay with you until he gets home?"

"No. I'm fine here. I'll go to the basement if the warning siren sounds. I'm worried about Josef."

"Josef is smart. He'll stay at the diner until it's safe to drive home. The road to the diner doesn't flood, so he'll be okay."

"What if a tree blows down and blocks the way?"

"Road crews will clear downed trees or set up a detour." He switched into the voice he used to calm nervous clients before they testified in court. "Don't make up scenarios to worry about. Nothing has happened. And if anything comes up, Josef will deal with it."

"You're right. Thank you, dear."

"I'm turning into the alley behind Sweets & Treats," Kurt said. "Clara's car is parked in her usual spot. She's at work, just like I said she'd be." *Like she always is, unless she's spending time with washboard-abs guy.*

"Good. Thank you, Kurt. I'm glad we can count on you."

"Always," Kurt said. He pulled into the spot next to Clara's. His wipers worked at their highest speed and couldn't keep up with the rain. "Make sure you've got your flashlight, your phone, and a water bottle handy. It's bad out here. I think you're going to have to take shelter in the basement."

CHAPTER 18

Kurt had his key ready as he ran to the back entrance to Sweets & Treats. He knocked once, calling Clara's name while reaching for the handle.

The door was unlocked and flew open; the wind ripping it from his hand and banging it against the wall. Kurt expended considerable force to shut it behind him. The workroom was empty.

"Clara," he called, racing into the front room.

She was nowhere to be seen. Clara's purse lay on the floor, her cell phone protruding from the top. Four cans of sparkling water sat on the countertop.

Dread crawled up his spine like a spider stalking its prey. He returned to the workroom and noticed the glass container wrapped in a towel and the bakery bag next to it.

"CLARA!" He realized the futility of his cry. She wasn't here, and something was wrong.

He went out the back door and fought his way to her car, hoping he'd find her there, waiting out the storm. Visibility had been so poor when he'd arrived that he wouldn't have seen her sitting there.

Clara's car was unlocked, but she wasn't inside.

The town's tornado warning siren activated and added itself to the roar of the storm. The wind swirled around him, catching him from every angle.

Kurt hunched over, shielding his face from the rain, as he staggered back to the rear entrance of the patisserie. He was reaching for the door when a furtive movement in the corner of his eye caught his attention.

He turned and cupped his hands around his eyes to get a better view.

A sodden four-legged creature approached him, picking up speed with each step.

Kurt recognized the bedraggled pup. He fell to one knee and opened his arms as Noelle leapt into them.

Clara was in trouble. Fear galvanized Kurt's resolve.

He pressed the dog to his chest. "Where's Clara?" he shouted to be heard above the wind.

Noelle wriggled out of his grasp, hit the pavement, and took off.

Kurt followed as Noelle made her way around the side of the building to the storefront. His heart fractured at the sight that greeted him. Clara was huddled in the deluge, propped against the wall of her shop. She'd gathered herself into a ball, except for her left leg, which stuck out. A ladder and the Sweets & Treats sign lay on the sidewalk nearby.

He was at her side in an instant.

"Clara," he said, his words whipped away by the wind. The sirens continued their dire warning. He put his hands on either side of her face.

"Kurt." He saw the word rather than heard it.

Noelle nestled herself against them.

He placed his mouth close to her ear. "Are you hurt?"

She nodded.

"We need to get inside."

She nodded again.

"I'm going to pick you up. If I hurt you, I'm sorry, but you can't stay here. Can you put your arms around my neck?"

Clara released her grip on her left arm and groaned when her left arm sagged, pain piercing her like a knife blade.

"Never mind," Kurt said. He moved her right hand back into position to support her left arm and stood. He gathered her into his arms, taking care not to touch her left leg, and lifted her.

The force of the wind made carrying her a Herculean task, but he didn't notice. The only thing on his mind was getting her to safety.

Kurt leaned against the side of the building for support while he fished his key out of his pocket. He approached the door from the side and inserted the key in the lock. The latch on the door gave way, and he brought Clara inside, Noelle on his heels.

He kicked the door shut behind him and crossed to the workroom, bending to set her gently under one of the sturdy tables. "If a tornado comes, we'll be safest away from the front window and under this table."

She nodded a third time, and her teeth chattered.

Kurt removed his rain-soaked jacket, then shoved it aside. "This won't do you any good." He cast his eyes around the room and spotted the stacks of clean aprons stacked by the sink. "Those will have to do."

He was halfway to the sink when a tremendous crack of lightning sounded, and the lights went out. Kurt used the flashlight on his cell phone to illuminate his path. He returned with the aprons in an instant.

Clara was shaking all over.

Kurt set the phone on the floor, its flashlight beam creating searchlight-like illumination. "Your left ankle is injured," Kurt said, unfolding an apron and wrapping it around her shoulders. "The way you groaned when you let go of your left arm tells me you've broken it or your collarbone."

"I… think… so," Clara said through her chattering teeth.

"You may be going into shock, too." He loosened the buttons of her shirt at the neck and draped additional aprons around her shoulders. "Are you headachy or nauseated?"

"No." She inhaled slowly as her shaking subsided. "I was cold from the rain. This is better."

"Good." He settled on the floor and pressed himself against her. "Lean on me," he said. "It takes a lot of energy to sit up with nothing against your back. You're not up to that right now."

Clara relaxed into him.

Rain hammered the roof, and wind whistled at the door.

Noelle sat facing them, wagging her tail.

"You, too, Noelle. I think you've had a traumatic time as well." Kurt patted his knee and Noelle curled up against it.

"We heard you shout," Clara said. "I yelled in response, but I knew you couldn't hear me." Her voice cracked. "I was so scared. I stayed calm at first, thinking someone would come along and find us. When the sirens went off, I knew that wasn't going to happen. Hearing your voice was like being thrown a lifeline. And when you didn't come out the front door…" Her words were lost in her tears.

"This brave girl heard me and ran around the building to find me." He rubbed Noelle's ears. "Just for the record—I knew you were here somewhere. I would not have left until I found you."

Clara cried harder. "I'm so… so very… sorry, Kurt."

"I guess working is the way you cope with things."

"No. I wasn't at the patisserie working. I came in to make you a surprise lunch. We planned to take it to you this afternoon at the cottage." She turned her face to his as far as she could until the pain shooting from her left shoulder caused her to stop. "There's a glass jar of béchamel sauce on the table above us to prove it."

"A what?"

"I was bringing you croque madame. Anyway, I was leaving

here when I heard the sign banging against the building, saw it was halfway down, and I went out to fix it." She closed her eyes. "And the rest, as they say, is history."

He fought the relief and hope surging through his veins. He'd seen her with that other guy only hours earlier. Maybe he'd drawn the wrong conclusion.

"I know it would have been a late lunch, but I'm working on a surprise project for… well… you, and that took more time this morning than I'd anticipated."

Kurt lost his battle against relief and hope and welcomed them.

"I need to apologize to you, Kurt. You were right last night. You mean the world to me, and I've been taking you for granted."

Kurt put a finger to her lips to silence her. "We've got time for that," he said. "We don't need to get into a deep relationship discussion while you're nursing broken bones."

"Okay. I agree I'm not at my best," she replied, "but I need you to know I love you."

He pressed a kiss against her temple. "I love you, too."

"I think the wind has died down," Clara said.

They listened.

"You're right. The rain's letting up." Kurt retrieved his phone and checked his weather app. "Time to get you to the emergency room."

"Can't I go home? If it's not better in the morning, I'll head to the hospital."

"No chance," he said. "You've got broken bones, and they won't be better in the morning. You'll be in too much pain to sleep. We're going. Now."

"What about Noelle?"

"We'll drop her off on our way."

"Okay. Feed her, too."

"Sure." Kurt eased himself away from her. "Can you sit up without help?"

As he stood up, Clara winced and clutched her left arm tighter to her chest.

"I'm going to back my truck to the door. I'll lift you into the passenger seat, get Noelle, and we'll be on our way."

He exited as the lights surged back on.

Kurt was back in moments and secured Clara and Noelle in his truck.

"One last thing," Clara said. "I noticed the compressors weren't running. Will you flip the breakers and set the alarm before we leave?"

Kurt attended to the final tasks. Her remembering them must mean she hadn't suffered a concussion in the fall. He was grateful for that.

CHAPTER 19

osef turned off the Johanson's sign and bolted the door. Relief washed over him as he observed the cars of his last two employees turn onto the highway, knowing they were headed away from the swirling mass of gray-green clouds bearing down on the diner.

He hurried through the restaurant to the rear door. The wind howled, and the rain came down in sheets. Hating the thought of Maisie weathering the storm alone, he considered getting into his car and driving home. But he'd be heading into it if he did that, and knew that wasn't an option.

The security door on the bakery building behind the diner swung wildly in the wind. Someone had forgotten to lock it, he thought in irritation. He pulled his keys from his pocket and opened the back door. He could be over and back in thirty seconds. The door was expensive, and he didn't want it to be blown off its hinges.

He had reached the bottom step of the stairs to the diner when he slipped. He lunged for the railing and grasped it, averting a fall. He bent against the wind and staggered toward the banging door.

The wind howled.

He continued on.

Halfway to his destination, he heard the terrifying telltale sound.

Josef abandoned his quest and reversed course, planting his feet against the wind with every step.

The sound, like a freight train, grew louder.

He was driven to his knees just steps away from the diner's back door. The wind kept him down, so he fought the rest of the way on hands and knees. He grasped the railing and pulled himself up the stairs, as if climbing a rope.

The rear door flew open when he released the latch, catching him squarely in the chest before the storm plastered it against the outside wall.

Josef threw himself inside the diner, giving up any thought of reaching out into the wind to grab the door and close it.

The train sounded like it was almost upon him. Wind and rain whipped around him from the open doorway.

Josef army-crawled along the floor to the windowless hallway between the kitchen and dining room. The men's restroom was the first door on his right. His best shot at surviving the tornado would be to take shelter there.

The bathroom door gave way to his shove. He crawled under a sink and curled into a ball, protecting his head with his hands.

The wind rattled and shook the structure. A deafening crack sounded, followed by the thud of debris landing on the roof. Glass shattered somewhere outside the door.

When asked about the experience later, Josef would say he felt he had huddled underneath the sink for hours. In reality, it had only been minutes.

The roaring receded, leaving behind the steady drum of rain on the roof.

Josef unwound his arms from his head and scooted out from

his nook. He rolled onto his knees and attempted to stand when a searing pain sliced through his chest like a knife.

Sinking onto his heels, he took two deep, painful breaths. He grasped the bowl of the sink and carefully pulled himself to his feet. The pain in his chest took his breath away. He clung to the sink to steady himself until the pain subsided.

Josef glanced at his reflection in the mirror. His skin was pale and perspiration dotted his upper lip. Now was not the time to have a heart attack, he thought.

He reached into his pocket for his phone and remembered leaving it on the counter by the rear door. He hoped it was still there.

Josef reached for the bathroom door and pulled it open, awakening the pain in his chest. The hallway was unchanged. He looked up. The ceiling was intact. The lights that had been on when he'd entered the bathroom were out, but everything else seemed fine. Josef made his way to the kitchen, keeping one hand pressed against the wall to steady himself.

The sight that greeted him in the kitchen was a different story. Water stood an inch deep on some parts of the floor. Debris had blown in from outside and was deposited every-where. A worktable had been turned on its side, and utensils, containers, and small appliances were strewn about. One large-paned window was missing, and rain poured inside.

He faced the door and narrowed his eyes against the early dusk. To his relief, his cell phone remained where he'd left it, untouched by the mayhem of the tornado.

Josef stepped over the sodden wreckage, holding onto any available surface. He picked up his phone. It still worked, but he had no signal.

His chest throbbed. He looked out the gaping hole where the rear door had been, and saw a pile of rubble where the bakery building used to be. The only thing that remained was the iron frame of the security door. The door itself and everything that had been behind the door was gone.

A wooden joist from the roof now lay on top of his car in the parking lot.

Josef turned and felt his way to the wall phone by the hostess desk. He needed to summon help for himself. The damage to his property was the least of his concerns. Josef hoped he had pulled a muscle in his chest, but he felt certain he was having a heart attack.

He picked up the receiver and his worst fears were confirmed. The line was dead.

CHAPTER 20

Kurt and Clara sat on molded plastic chairs in the waiting area of the hospital's emergency room. The intake nurse had told them to expect a five-hour wait and advised them to stake a claim on chairs in the waiting room as soon as she sent them back. They got busy after storms, and it would soon be standing room only.

The place was packed, just as the nurse had predicted.

"I can't believe they're going to leave you sitting here—in pain—for five hours." Kurt scowled at a man in hospital scrubs pushing a woman in a wheelchair.

"If I keep my left arm immobilized," Clara replied, "it doesn't hurt. My ankle's getting sore though."

Kurt got onto one knee and gingerly lifted the bottom of her pant leg. "It's swelling. I think we'd better get you out of your shoe."

Clara nodded.

"I'm afraid to say, it will hurt."

"I'll be all right. You'll have to do it for me."

Kurt untied and loosened the laces of her left sneaker.

She took a deep breath and held it as he eased off the shoe, followed by her short sock.

He looked up at her. "Breathe," he reminded her as he slipped back into his seat. "I'm sorry. That was bad."

Clara released the breath she was holding. "It's better now."

The low volume of hushed conversation in the waiting room was interrupted by blaring announcements from the hospital's public address system.

Clara closed her eyes and leaned her head against the wall behind her. She and Kurt listened to the cheerful banter of the game show playing on the television hanging on the opposite wall. A series of staccato beeps caused her to open her eyes.

Kurt leaned forward in his chair.

A local news anchor appeared on the screen in front of a backdrop that proclaimed Breaking News. "This just in," the woman said. "An EF5 tornado hit Pinewood for the first time on record. The twister touched down ten minutes ago."

The screen changed to footage of wind and rain.

"Our crew is traveling to the scene, but downed power lines and trees have blocked their path. We'll have footage as soon as it's available. Reports from the Pinewood Springs Motel tell us the twister passed on the ground between the motel and Johanson's Diner."

Kurt gripped the handles of his chair, and Clara gasped.

"We've had no reports of injuries. The motel is intact. Visibility is poor and the manager can't see if the landmark diner is still standing. Stay tuned for further updates. We now return you to your regular programming."

"Thank God Maisie and Josef aren't at the diner on Sundays," Clara said. "But what about the staff—or customers?"

She looked at Kurt. The color had drained from his face.

"Oh, no..."

He nodded. "Josef went to the diner to send everyone home and shut it down."

"Maisie?"

"She stayed home."

"Call her. Hopefully, he got home before the twister hit."

Kurt was already pulling his phone from his pocket when it began ringing with Maisie's ringtone.

"You okay?"

"It's Josef," Maisie said in a voice laden with fear. "He was at the diner."

Clara leaned toward Kurt.

He angled the phone away from his ear so she could hear Maisie.

"You've seen the news?" he asked.

"Yes. I called him, but he didn't answer." Her voice cracked.

"Cell service is probably out," Kurt said, forcing down his own rising panic. "He may already be on the way home."

"What if he isn't?"

"You heard what the motel manager said. He thinks it went between his property and the diner."

"He can't know that." Maisie began to cry.

Clara looked into Kurt's eyes. "Go." She mouthed the word.

Kurt swiveled his eyes to take in the waiting room.

"I'm fine," Clara said softly as Maisie continued to sob. "They'll take me back when it's my turn and nothing you do here will speed that up for me."

He nodded.

"Go find Josef." Clara was firm.

"I'm on my way to the diner. I'll track him down." He pressed the phone to his ear. "I'll call as soon as I have news, but don't worry if you don't hear from me for a while. As I said, cell service must be out in that area."

"Be careful, Kurt," Maisie said. "I don't want you to risk yourself."

"The storm has passed. I'll be fine." He disconnected the call.

"You're sure?" he asked Clara, touching her cheek. "I hate leaving you like this."

"I'm positive. Now get out of here. And keep me posted. I'll recover from this." She glanced down at herself. "We can't lose Josef."

Kurt kissed her forehead, then stood and wove his way out of the packed waiting room.

Clara continued to watch until he disappeared from her sight.

The Breaking News banner slashed across the television screen and the anchor reappeared. "Our film crews just arrived. Here's a first look at the damage."

The camera showed the Johanson's Diner sign hanging by a single support, then panned to the devastation behind it.

Clara uttered a strangled cry. The bakery building was now a pile of rubble. She closed her eyes and prayed that Josef was safe.

CHAPTER 21

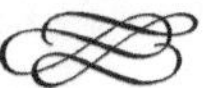

Kurt headed for the highway that ran by the motel and diner. City streets would have been faster, but every one of the prospective routes went through heavily wooded areas of the aptly named Pinewood. He couldn't risk the delay a downed tree would cause.

He approached the familiar exit, leaning forward to peer out the patch of windshield cleared by his wipers. The light above the exit sign was out.

He left the highway and turned right at the bottom of the ramp. The long L-shaped form of the Pinewood Springs Motel was to the left. He swung his SUV to the right and his headlights picked out Johanson's Diner.

Kurt drove through the customer parking lot in front of the diner as if on a slalom course, driving around shingles, wooden beams, and a mangled oven from the bakery building.

He parked when he could go no farther and dashed to the door, dodging the sign that still blew in the wind. The door was locked, and he fumbled in his wallet for the spare key Josef had pressed on him years ago. "Just in case," the older man had said.

Kurt pulled the key from between two rarely used credit cards and brought it to the lock. He successfully inserted the key and the door swung open.

"Josef," Kurt yelled, striding into the building. "*Josef.*"

Josef responded with a muffled groan.

"JOSEF!"

"In back," came the halting reply.

Kurt felt his way through the pitch black hallway to the kitchen.

Josef stood, bent over the sink, his arms hugging his sides.

As Kurt crossed to him, Josef leaned over and dry heaved into the sink.

Kurt put his arms around the older man to steady him.

Josef winced at his touch.

"Did you get hurt?"

Josef shook his head. "Chest pain," he whispered. "Tried to call…"

"Don't talk." Kurt ran his hand over Josef's clammy forehead, then down his arm to check his pulse. "I'm taking you to the hospital. Your pulse is regular, but you need to be checked out. Now."

Josef nodded.

Kurt positioned Josef's arm over his shoulders. "I'm going to carry you."

Josef shook his head no. "If you help me, I can walk."

Kurt supported Josef's weight against himself, and the two men inched their way to Kurt's SUV.

"Call Maisie," Josef uttered between clenched teeth.

"We haven't got service out here. I'll call when we get to the hospital." He spun his SUV onto the deserted highway and stepped on the gas. "I talked to her before I came out here. She's home and is fine. The tornado didn't come close to the down-town area."

Josef's sigh sounded of relief rather than pain.

They zoomed along the highway at speeds that would have

landed Kurt in jail if the highway patrol had stopped him. His phone rang as he took the hospital exit.

"Did you find him?" If Clara's voice had been kindling, it would have been on the verge of bursting into flame.

"Yes. We're on our way to the hospital. We should be there in under five minutes."

"Is he hurt?" By now, her tone was a roaring fire.

"That's what we're going to find out. Are you still in the waiting room?"

"Yes."

"Call Maisie. Tell her I'll pick her up after I drop Josef off."

"Will do."

THE CALL DISCONNECTED, and Clara dialed Maisie's number. She closed her eyes, fighting against the tears that threatened to consume her, as she listened to it ring before clicking over to voicemail.

Clara dialed again, with the same result. Alarm bells rang so loudly in Clara's head that she swore the people seated around her could hear them. Maisie would be glued to her phone, waiting for news, unless something was wrong.

She scrolled through her contacts and dialed Laura. Tabitha and Maisie were dear friends, and she knew Laura loved Maisie.

She answered on the first ring. Laura, Tabitha, and Ian were gathered around the television in the living room, watching the horrific images of the damage caused by the tornado. "Everything okay, Clara? Ian said he saw Kurt bring Noelle home during the storm and then take off again."

"I'm sitting in the ER waiting room, with a sprained ankle and likely a broken arm or collarbone."

"Oh, no! What happened?"

"I'll fill you in later. I'm calling because I'm worried about Maisie." Clara supplied the scant facts that she knew.

"I'll drive over there right now," Laura said, shoving her feet into her shoes. "When I find her, I'll let you know, and I'll bring her to the hospital." She hurried through the kitchen and plucked her purse from its hook by her back door.

"Go with your mother," Tabitha said to Ian. "I'd come, too, but I'd slow you down."

Ian nodded and raced after his mother. If something was wrong with Maisie, he wanted to help.

CHAPTER 22

 lara closed her eyes to block the images of the televised storm report. A seven-car pile-up had occurred on the highway on the other side of town and trees had crashed through the roofs of three two-story houses close to the diner. The announcer had commented on how lucky it had been that the storm had hit before bedtime. No one had been asleep in their second-floor bedroom when the trees broke through.

The sounds of approaching sirens blared without interruption. Flashing red and blue lights cascaded across the automatic sliding glass doors at the entrance to the emergency room.

She offered up prayers for Maisie and Josef on a continuous loop. They'd become like parents to her, and she wouldn't allow the thought that something had happened to both of them.

Clara heard the whoosh as the automatic doors opened, followed by a voice she knew and loved. Despite the pain that stabbed through her shoulder, Clara turned her head far enough to see Kurt pushing a wheelchair toward the same intake nurse who had helped Clara earlier.

Josef sat, doubled over, his hands on his knees as if to prevent himself from falling to the floor.

Clara rocked forward. She wanted to get up and join them. She rose on her right leg, but the moment her left foot touched the floor, she cried out in pain and sank back into her chair.

The intake nurse pointed to a door on her left, then disappeared from view.

Kurt steered the chair to the door.

The nurse opened it and both men disappeared from view.

Clara forcefully exhaled the breath she'd been holding. Whatever was wrong with Josef, the intake nurse thought it serious enough to take him directly into treatment. She was thankful he didn't have to sit for hours in the waiting room, like she was doing.

Time dragged for Clara until Laura called to report that Maisie had unknowingly turned her phone to silent and missed their calls. They were en route to the hospital and would be there in minutes. Laura planned to drop Maisie and Ian at the door while she parked her car.

The next time the automatic doors opened, Maisie stepped into view, clutching Ian's elbow to steady herself.

Clara released her grip on her left arm to wave to them and instantly regretted it, abandoning her effort mid-wave.

Ian had seen her anyway, and steered Maisie over to her. "Have you heard anything?" Maisie asked.

"No. Kurt hasn't come out. They must be letting him stay with Josef." Clara spoke to Ian. "Take Maisie to the intake nurse at the middle window. She's the one who admitted Josef. Tell her his wife is here and wants to be with her husband."

Ian nodded and helped the older woman to the window.

Clara watched the scene at the window play out. The nurse recognized Maisie and greeted her like a beloved member of her family. No surprise, Clara thought. Everyone in Pinewood knew and loved Maisie and Josef.

Maisie sailed through the door to the treatment area on Ian's arm.

Laura came through the automatic doors just as Kurt and Ian reentered the waiting room. They all converged on Clara.

"Any news?" Clara asked.

Kurt rubbed his hand over tired eyes. "When I got to Josef, he thought he was having a heart attack."

Laura and Clara gasped in unison.

"His pulse was steady, but I was concerned. I decided to drive him here. The intake nurse took us right back immediately, and he was the center of attention." Kurt chuckled. "If Pinewood has local celebrities, it's those two. Anyway, it seems Josef's chest was bruised by flying debris. He took shelter inside the diner seconds before the tornado hit the bakery building."

"So that's it? A bruise?" Laura asked.

Kurt shook his head. "The real culprit—what was making him so sick—was a gallbladder attack. The doctor said it can mimic a heart attack. They're running additional tests to confirm, but the doctor is admitting him tonight for surgery in the morning."

Laura brought her hand to her heart. "That's a relief. I didn't know he'd been having trouble."

"He told the doctor he hasn't had any symptoms—until today."

"Will Maisie stay with him tonight?" Clara asked.

"She wants to, but he won't hear of it."

"Take her home when she's ready to go," Clara said.

"What about you?" Kurt dropped to one knee in front of her. "Are you still waiting to be seen?"

"Unfortunately, yes."

"That's horrible, sweetheart. I'm so sorry."

"I'm tired of waiting, but I keep reminding myself how lucky I am that I wasn't one of those brought in by ambulance."

A person in scrubs stepped into the waiting room and called Clara's name.

"Speak of the devil," Clara said.

Kurt helped her to her feet. "Tell the attendant we'll need a wheelchair," Kurt said to Ian.

The boy jumped to the task.

"I'm so glad we came," Laura said. "Ian and I will wait for Clara until we know if she's being admitted or released. We'll take her home if she's released. Kurt can stay here with Maisie."

Kurt guided Clara into the wheelchair. "I don't want to leave you."

"You're not. I'm in good hands with Laura and Ian. I want you with Josef and Maisie." She turned her face to his. "Promise me you'll come see me tomorrow."

Kurt brushed a kiss along her temple and whispered, "I promise. And I'll call you tonight."

The attendant whisked her away.

Laura spotted three chairs together in the waiting room. They settled themselves in to wait.

Ian was the first to speak. "Was the bakery building destroyed?"

"Demolished. It took a direct hit from the tornado."

Ian's shoulders sagged.

"It'll be okay," Kurt said. "They weren't using it for much anymore."

Ian's eyes grew wide. "That's Maisie's new cooking school. Good Food - Great Life."

"You know about that?" Kurt asked.

"Know about it?" Laura laughed as she reached over and mussed her son's mop of hair. "It's all he's talked about. He took her first class and then signed up for everything she's teaching. He's becoming quite the cook."

"Really?"

Ian nodded. "They're fun. I've learned a ton."

"I can vouch for that," Laura said. "We've been eating like kings since that class."

"And now it's gone," Ian said, dejection filling every syllable. "Does Maisie know?"

"The only thing she could think about was Josef," Kurt said, leaning back in his chair. "But losing that building doesn't have to be the end of her school. I know how much it means to her." He gazed at Ian. "And you."

A smile forced its way around the tired lines at Kurt's mouth. "I've got the perfect location for Good Food - Great Life when Maisie's ready to reopen."

CHAPTER 23

Noelle heard the familiar footsteps on the walkway to Clara's cottage. She sprang off the sofa, where she had been glued to Clara's side, and raced to the front door. Noelle alternated between pawing at the door and crouching into downward dog with her tail waving like a flag in an offshore breeze.

Kurt raised his hand to knock when Clara called, "Come on in."

He opened the screen door and stepped into the living room. "Are you in the habit of welcoming people into your home without knowing who they are?"

"Noelle would have been barking her head off if you were a stranger. Besides—you texted ten minutes ago that you were on your way over."

"Still—the door was unlocked. That's not safe."

"I unlocked it after you called." Clara held out both arms to him. "Stop fussing. Come over here and kiss me."

Kurt gladly complied.

"Join me," Clara said as she patted the cushion next to her.

Kurt lowered himself to the sofa as Noelle launched herself onto it and reclaimed her spot.

Kurt and Clara laughed in unison. Clara pulled her faithful pup onto her lap.

Kurt sank into the deep cushions.

"Tired?" Clara asked.

He nodded. "It's been a long twenty-four hours."

"I'll say. But with good results for everyone. Thank you for letting me know that Josef's surgery went well this morning. Is Maisie still with him?"

"I dropped her off at home for a nap on my way here. We stayed at the hospital until Josef was moved into a room. She only agreed to leave him when I promised to bring her back to the hospital later."

"I'm glad to hear it. I know she was up late last night because I woke this morning to a series of group texts from Maisie to Joan, Betty, and me that were sent after midnight. She let them know about my injuries and the fact that I would be unable to work for a few weeks. At one point, she even suggested they bar the doors if I tried to get in. The three of them divvied up my work for the next three weeks. They assured me they'd take care of Sweets & Treats."

"That sounds like them." He looked into her eyes. "How do you feel about that—leaving Sweets & Treats in their hands for a few weeks?"

Clara pursed her lips in thought. "I'm grateful—of course—to have capable and willing employees. But my first thought was 'no way—I'm not going to be out that long.' That was when I was still in bed. I got up and everything hurt. My mind wants to work, but my body says no."

"I had that same internal conversation with myself when I played college football. I told the coach I could play after an injury. Thank goodness he recognized testosterone-fueled idiocy and didn't allow it."

"Laura came down to check on me this morning. She brought my breakfast and left a sandwich in the fridge for lunch. She also helped me change my clothes and hobble out here."

"How's your ankle?" He looked at it, elevated on an ottoman with an ice pack wrapped around it. "You said it's only a sprain."

"A minor one, at that. Icing and elevating my foot has helped a lot. I was able to put weight on it when I went to the bathroom a while ago. It's sore, but not painful."

"That's good to hear."

"I've got a hairline crack in my left collarbone. If I keep my arm in this sling, it doesn't hurt. The doctor said I bruised my hand, my knee, and my bum in the fall. She said I would be sore all over and recommended taking anti-inflammatories around the clock for the next few days."

"Do you have those?"

"Laura brought me a bottle of aspirin when she came back a few minutes ago with that stack of fall decor magazines and the last two books selected by her book club."

Kurt feigned surprise. "Clara Conway is going to sit around with her feet up, reading?"

"Hard to believe, but true. The doctor told me the collarbone should heal in three weeks. My ankle may be faster. She told me to be patient—to allow my body to mend. If I jump the gun and go back too early, I run the risk of re-injuring myself and delaying my recovery." Clara chuckled. "And she recommended I stay off of ladders during thunderstorms."

"Smart doctor," Kurt grinned. "I'm glad you're going to heed her advice."

"The events of the last day have brought a lot of things into focus for me. We're a tight-knit group—you, me, Maisie, Josef, Laura, Tabitha, and Ian." She paused, thinking. "I'd add my bakery crew, too. We're like an extended family. I've never been part of something like this, but I want it. Very much."

Kurt nodded, encouraging her to continue.

"I felt like it was all up to me to make Sweets & Treats a success. Investing my entire inheritance in the patisserie made me feel like I'd be letting my mother down if it failed. That string of text messages made me realize that Maisie, Betty, and Joan are as committed as I am." She pinched the bridge of her nose to block her tears. "My dreams and investment are safe with them while I step away to heal."

"They are. I know how it feels to be responsible for a business. When I started my law firm after Rachel died, I threw myself into my work. I thought if I was too busy to think, the pain would go away. That didn't happen. Instead, things got worse. So, I worked even harder. I struggled to bring in clients and was consumed with worry about making payroll or laying people off."

"What changed? Did you have a broken collarbone, sprained ankle experience?"

Kurt chuckled. "Mine was a bleeding ulcer. It forced me to slow down. The other members of the firm stepped up and before I knew it, we were bringing in so much work I had to hire an associate. We've continued to grow ever since."

Kurt took her hand in his. "Sweets & Treats is going to be a tremendous success. I'm certain of it. It may not happen next week—or this summer—or even this year, but you'll look back and wonder why you ever doubted it."

"I'm going with that." She brought his hand to her lips and kissed it. "I want to tell you what I'd planned to say yesterday afternoon at Bloom Cottage."

Clara locked eyes with him. "Kurt, the most important thing in my life is 'us.' I don't want any of this without you. I took you for granted. That was stupid. I shouldn't have done that—and I won't do it again."

He squeezed her hand.

"I was going to ask you to let me make it up to you—to give us a second chance."

"I hope you know the answer to that is yes."

"After you swooped in like my knight-in-shining-armor last night, I was hoping…"

"I overreacted to your falling asleep in the movie. It happens to all of us. When I saw you leaving that guy's house… well," he sighed heavily.

"I'm not seeing some other guy! He's part of your surprise—which won't be one if I tell you about it. You believe me, don't you?"

"Yes. Of course. And when I laid eyes on you, curled up and hurt outside Sweets & Treats in the storm? I knew. I love you, Clara. Nothing's going to change that."

He leaned in and kissed her for a long time.

They pulled apart for air. "I love you too," Clara said. "I'm afraid dates will have to be right here, on my sofa, for a while," she said. "At least I'll be on time."

"Suits me just fine," he replied. "I've cleared my calendar this week, except for a hearing on Thursday. I'll drive Maisie everywhere she needs to go. Josef will be released from the hospital in a few days, so I'll bring him home. I want to check on my rental properties after the storm. And," he looked at her with a twinkle in his eye, "I have an idea about a new location for Good Food - Great Life."

"Oh, Kurt! That's wonderful. What're you thinking?"

He checked his watch. "I need to go. My maintenance crew is meeting me in fifteen minutes. I'll bring us takeout for dinner, and I'll fill you in then."

"Fine, but I can't believe you're going to leave me hanging."

"You'll just have to be patient," he teased. "Choose the restaurant and place the order for pickup at six."

"Will do," Clara said.

He leaned in and kissed her again.

Noelle walked him to the door, her tail signaling her approval of the conversation she'd overheard.

CHAPTER 24

Clara settled into the Adirondack chair nestled under a tree in the patch of lawn behind her cottage. She'd managed the two steps back and forth to the kitchen to set herself up with a thermos of coffee, her laptop, and phone. What a difference a week made, she thought. She wouldn't have been able to navigate the steps when her sprained ankle was new.

She took a sip of her coffee and rested her head against the back of the chair. The sun was high in a cloudless sky. The weather had been gorgeous since the horrible day of the tornado. She was grateful to sit outside and enjoy the sunshine.

Noelle sniffed the dandelions in the yard. She poked her nose into one that had gone to seed, and it exploded into a cloud of wispy tendrils. Noelle sneezed so violently that it almost knocked her off her paws. She looked at Clara as if to say, "What was that?"

Clara laughed, and Noelle got the zoomies, racing from one corner of the yard to the other.

Clara opened her laptop and turned her attention to the recipes she was editing for Maisie. She'd offered to help her business partner with the collection of recipes she planned to hand out to her students at Good Food - Great Life. Since Maisie had taken over Clara's duties at the patisserie during her recovery, it seemed only fair.

Clara perused an entry for meatloaf stroganoff. It was Josef's favorite, and Clara could personally attest to how tasty it was. She made sure to accurately abbreviate the words tablespoon and teaspoon, adding periods after them. Being an editor meant attending to every tiny detail. Assuring consistency in a cookbook was a bigger task than Clara had imagined. She'd already made dozens—if not hundreds—of corrections. Her goal today was to complete editing so she could begin formatting. She bent over her laptop and worked uninterrupted until mid afternoon.

Clara's phone rang as she finished a turkey chili recipe that sounded delicious. She'd never used white beans in her own version and decided she should try them. "Hey, Ian."

Noelle, who lay snoozing in the grass at her feet, lifted her head at the sound of his name.

"How're you doing?" Clara asked. "Your biggest fan is ready for her walk."

"I'm sorry. I won't have time to take her today."

"That's okay. She'll live. What's going on?"

"Today is our day to take dinner to Maisie and Josef."

"The meal train, right?"

"Yep. Mom had it all planned. Except she needed to take Granny to the dentist. She broke a tooth, and it hurts so the dentist is squeezing her in. Mom just called and they're still waiting to be seen."

"I'm sorry to hear that. Toothaches are miserable."

"Mom said we'll bring takeout to Maisie and Josef if she's not home in time to cook." Clara heard him inhale before he continued. "I wondered if I could make the dinner. For us to take."

"That's an excellent idea! What was your mom going to fix?"

"I don't know. She didn't leave a recipe out on the counter."

"Can you call her to ask?"

"I kinda wanna surprise Mom, too."

Clara grinned. "You're a thoughtful young man, Ian. I can try to help. What ingredients do you have on hand?"

"There's a two-pound package of ground beef in the fridge. We have a big bag of redskin potatoes on the counter. Mom bought mushrooms, parsley, and green beans at the farmers market."

Clara scrolled to an earlier screen. "Do you have eggs?"

"Yeah. We always have eggs."

"How about an onion?"

"We've got one of those, too."

"Breadcrumbs? Sour cream?" She heard the refrigerator door open.

"There's no sour cream. I don't know where to look for breadcrumbs."

"No worries. I have both." She gathered her laptop and got to her feet. "We're going to make Maisie's famous meatloaf stroganoff. I was just editing the recipe for her cookbook. It's Josef's favorite, too."

"I'm not sure I know how…."

"I'm going to teach you. You'll do the actual cooking. I'm not up to standing for long periods yet, but I'll be your advisor."

"You're sure I can do this?"

"Positive. I've watched you in the kitchen. You have a knack for it." She slowly climbed the steps to her kitchen. "I can walk to your house, no problem. But I don't think I can do it carrying my laptop with the recipe, plus the sour cream and breadcrumbs."

"I'll be right down," he said. His enthusiasm was palpable. "Can Noelle come with us?"

"I'm sure she'd love that. I'll be waiting for you in the kitchen."

They disconnected the call.

"Come on, girl," Clara said to Noelle. "I don't know about you, but I'm getting cabin fever. We've been home for over a week. We're not going far, but at least it's not here. And it'll be so much fun to help Ian."

CHAPTER 25

*L*aura and Tabitha entered the kitchen.

Ian looked up from the stove where he was whisking a mixture of milk and sour cream, thickened with cornstarch, into a mushroom-infused broth. He set down his whisk and moved to his great-grandmother's side.

"Whatever you're making smells marvelous," Tabitha said. "You don't need to help me. I'm fine. At least I will be until the Novocain wears off. What're you making?"

"Meatloaf stroganoff," Ian said, his voice vibrating with excitement. "It's Josef's favorite."

"My goodness," Laura said. "That sounds better than what I had planned."

"We've got mashed potatoes and green beans, too," Ian added. "See that parsley drying on the paper towels by the sink? We're using that as garnish."

"How lovely, my boy," Tabitha said. "Well done."

Laura looked at Ian, her eyebrows arching like they were about to jump the high hurdles. "I had no idea you knew how to make all this."

He gave his sauce a final stir and turned off the burner. "I didn't. Clara helped me."

"I advised you—that's my only contribution. Your son—and great-grandson—made the creamiest mashed potatoes I've ever tasted." She addressed the boy. "I can't wait for Maisie to see what you've done and to taste your version of her recipe."

Tabitha clapped. Ian flushed as Clara and his mother joined in.

"I'm glad we don't have to bring them takeout, after all. The whole idea of a meal train is to supply home-cooked dinners."

"We had enough to make two meat loafs," Ian said. "Clara said it'll make terrific sandwiches for Josef's lunch tomorrow."

"The best," Clara chimed in.

"We'd better get the food to the car. I don't want to be late," Laura said. She rummaged in the pantry and emerged with two large, double-handled grocery bags.

"I'm going to leave you to it and head for my chair by the front window," Tabitha said.

"Do you want us to leave some of this for your dinner?" Laura asked.

Tabitha shook her head. "My jaw is aching. A cup of tea and broth will be fine."

"I'll fix it as soon as we get home after dropping this off."

"No rush. I'm not the least bit hungry," Tabitha said as she left the kitchen.

Noelle followed on her heels. The old woman who had feared dogs her entire life had formed an unbreakable bond with the small pup.

Clara rose and helped Ian place the potatoes in a disposable container.

"Come with us, Clara. I'm sure Maisie and Josef would love to see you," Laura said.

Clara paused, a tong full of green beans poised over the open mouth of a Pyrex storage container. "I haven't seen Josef since he got home from the hospital. I'd love to."

"We won't stay long. I know he's still recovering. We'll drop off the food, say hello, and be out of there in a flash."

"Sounds like a plan." Clara lifted the remaining beans from the pan and placed them in the container.

Ian put them on top of the stacked plastic containers in one of the grocery bags. "That's everything," he said.

He and Laura carried the food while Clara trailed behind them. They made the short drive to Maisie and Josef's house and were soon unpacking their offerings.

Maisie was inspecting Ian's handiwork when Josef appeared in the doorway. "That's meatloaf stroganoff," he said, sniffing the air. "I'd know it anywhere."

Maisie turned her head over her shoulder to speak to him. "It sure is," she said, "and by the looks of it, it's better than mine." She smiled at Ian as he hovered over her shoulder. "I may have to retire this recipe from my repertoire after this," she teased.

Ian's normally ruddy complexion grew redder.

"Clara!" Josef cried. "I didn't see you there. How are you, my dear?"

"Better every day." She crossed the kitchen and leaned in to kiss his cheek. "You?"

"Same. We'll both be back to normal soon."

"I hope so. I'm getting antsy, sitting around my house all day long."

"Right?" Josef warmed to the subject. "I wanted to take a ride out to the diner—just to see how the cleanup of the bakery building site was going. I even promised to remain seat-belted in the car. Maisie and Kurt wouldn't consider it."

"This is my first outing," Clara said. "I feel like an escaped prisoner."

"Now you know what it was like for me when I was recovering from my stroke," Maisie said. She looked at Ian. "Move the food into the dining room, please. I'll grab silverware for every-one. It's time we had a big family meal again."

"The food is for you," Laura protested. "We'll get out of your hair."

"Nonsense," Maisie said. "You heard that husband of mine. He's starved for company. You've brought enough for an army. Let's enjoy this while it's still hot."

Laura looked at Clara.

Clara shrugged. "I've never won an argument against these two. I'd advise you not to try."

Kurt pulled up as food and silverware were being ferried to the table. He entered through the back door and stepped into the hubbub in the kitchen.

"Kurt," Maisie cried. "Now the gang's all here. Will you be a dear and fill a pitcher with water for the table?"

"Yes, ma'am," he said, doing as she asked, a puzzled expression on his face. "What's going on?"

"Dinner," came Maisie's one-syllable reply. "Join us. We've got plenty."

"It's your meatloaf, right?" He asked, sniffing the air as he ran water into the pitcher.

She nodded.

"You weren't supposed to cook."

"I didn't," she said. "Ian made it."

"Wow. I guess what you told me about him is true."

"I'm so sad I can't continue my classes," she replied. "He was my best pupil."

Kurt turned off the faucet and followed her into the dining room. He placed the pitcher on the table and slid into the empty chair next to Clara.

They joined hands as Josef said grace, then passed dishes and filled plates. The room was quiet except for the sounds of cutlery scraping plates and water glasses tinkling as they tucked into the meal.

Maisie broke the silence, thanking Laura and Ian for the excellent meal, and praising Ian for his skillful execution of her recipe. Everyone else at the table joined in.

"Maisie tells me you're her star student." Kurt turned to Ian, who was still blushing from the compliments he'd received. "Would you like to take more classes?"

"Sure," he said. "I signed up for all of them."

"They're not going to happen now," Maisie said, unable to keep the disappointment out of her voice. "But you're welcome here for private lessons, if you'd like."

"We wouldn't dream of putting you out," Laura began before Kurt held up a hand to stop her.

"I've got a better idea. I've found a new home for Good Food - Great Life."

"We owned the building behind the diner, so we didn't have any expenses there other than utilities," Maisie said. "My fledgeling cooking school isn't making enough to pay rent." Her voice was tinged with sadness.

"I know a landlord who won't charge you rent until you're firmly in the black."

Maisie rolled her eyes. "You can't give me property for free, Kurt. Besides, you don't have any vacancies."

"I will, as of the first of the month. The pharmacy in the block next to Sweets & Treats is going out of business. The pharmacist sold his prescriptions to a chain, and he's closing his doors."

"Won't you rent it to someone who can pay you?" Josef asked.

"It's not that simple," Kurt said. "The market is tough right now. Brick-and-mortar stores are shrinking. Other than a certain patisserie owner"—he turned his head to smile at Clara—"I haven't had any inquiries from tenants seeking downtown retail space for months." He looked from Josef to Maisie. "If you go into that spot, I know it will be properly maintained. It's close to Sweets & Treats, so the two of you can join forces for promotions and events. And you'll bring people into downtown, which will benefit my other tenants." He leaned back in his chair. "You'd be doing me a favor. We'll work out a sliding scale of rental payments for when you become profitable. And I'm confident you will."

Clara's eyes shone as she took Kurt's hand and squeezed it.

Maisie looked at Josef.

He nodded in answer to her unspoken question.

She rose and came around the table to where Kurt sat, throwing her arms around his neck. "Thank you, dear boy," she whispered.

Kurt blinked rapidly while Maisie and Clara allowed their happy tears to flow.

"When the bakery building was destroyed, I kept telling myself that God had a better plan for your school, Maisie," Josef said. "Now we know what the Almighty had in mind."

CHAPTER 26

Clara drained the last sip of coffee from her mug and set it in the sink. She'd finished formatting Maisie's *Recipes and Rules: How Good Food Makes a Great Life* and had imported into the manuscript the photos Susan had taken. The book was now posted on the cooking school's website. It looked fabulous. She intended to talk to Maisie about publishing print copies to sell in Sweets & Treats and the independent bookstore downtown. Clara smiled to herself. This was the type of collaboration Kurt had envisioned.

She walked through the small house, casting about for a project to sink her teeth into. What she really wanted to do was go back to Sweets & Treats. Her ankle felt fine. She knew she was ready, but she and Josef had made a pact that they'd obey doctor's orders to the letter. For both of them, that meant three weeks off work. They had one more week left. She'd keep her promise.

She opened her medicine cabinet and peered at the labels of her stash of over-the-counter medications. Purging expired items was in order. She pulled her trash can from under the sink and got busy. In twenty minutes, she'd listed the items she needed to replace, wiped the shelves, and stashed the bag of expired items in her car for disposal at the hospital.

Clara folded her lips into a thin line. She'd finished the magazines and the book club books Laura had brought her. She'd gone through her closet the day before. Two large garbage bags full of clothes stood by her back door, ready to be donated. If she didn't find something to do, she'd lose her mind.

Clara's phone rang with a call from Kurt while she was headed for her pantry.

"Hi, sweetheart. Am I disturbing you?"

"Not in the least."

"Good. I have a favor to ask. If you've got time."

"I've got nothing but. What's up?"

"I just got a call from the supervisor of the crew installing my kitchen at Bloom Cottage. He's got a bunch of questions. I'm tied up in court until late this afternoon—and I don't think I know the answers, anyway."

"What about your kitchen designer? I'm sure she can help them."

Kurt was silent.

"The woman you hired to put your plans together for you?" Clara prompted.

"Actually," Kurt hesitated before he continued. "I never hired her."

"Oh. Then what plans are they using?"

"Remember those drawings you made when we were at the cottage before construction started?"

"Kurt—those were literally on the back of napkins."

"I know. I took them to the office and photocopied them for the construction crew." He sounded sheepish. "They looked as good as her proposals. And you're an expert. I knew you'd set it up perfectly." He didn't add that, even then, he'd hoped she would become the lady of the house one day.

"I know how I'd want it set up, but I'm not a professional."

"Well… they're working from your drawings. And they have questions. Would you mind talking to my supervisor?"

"Sure. I'm happy to do that, but I don't know what you'd choose."

"That's easy—I want what you want."

"Then give him my phone number. And you can't complain if you don't like my ideas."

"That won't happen. I'll text you his name and call him now."

Clara heard someone call Kurt's name.

"We're back in session. I've got to go. Thank you, sweetheart." He disconnected the call.

Clara stared at her phone, trying to remember the details of the kitchen design she'd sketched on those napkins.

Her phone buzzed with Kurt's text, followed by an incoming call from the supervisor. After five minutes of back-and-forth conversation, they agreed they should continue their discussion in person at the cottage. Clara needed to see what he was describing.

"I've got time now," Clara responded to his question.

"Kurt told me you're not driving yet, after your accident," he said. "I'm in town buying another bag of grout. I'll pick you up and run you back home when we're done."

"Thanks," Clara said. She gave him her address. She was about to end the call when an idea flashed through her mind. "Can I hire you to do something for me? It involves Bloom Cottage—and it's a surprise for Kurt."

"How could I say no to that?"

Clara told him about the swing she'd had made for the porch. "The woodworker called yesterday to tell me it's finished. He agreed to hold the swing for me until I'm driving again, but it would be wonderful if we grabbed it, and you installed it on the front porch."

"Is that what those bolts in the ceiling are for?"

"Yes. I'll show you the photo I have of Kurt as a kid on his grandparent's old swing. I had it replicated."

"I can't wait to see it," the supervisor said. "We'll make sure it's securely in place. I'll pick you up in ten minutes."

Clara whistled for Noelle and shooed her through the back door to do her business. "I'm going out, and I'm not sure when I'll be back."

Noelle obeyed her mistress and returned in a flash.

"Good girl." Clara shut and locked the door. "I'm going to convince Kurt we need to take a ride into the country tomorrow—to check on the decisions I made for his kitchen."

Noelle lifted her soulful eyes to Clara.

"But we're really going there to show Kurt the swing." She bent and ruffled Noelle's ears. "Do you want to come with us?"

Noelle woofed and swept her tail against the floor.

"I thought you would." Clara kissed the top of Noelle's head. "You need to be part of this memory."

CHAPTER 27

"Thank you for forcing me to leave my office by noon," Kurt said, glancing at Clara.

"No one should work past noon on Saturday," she said.

"You do."

"Unless you're a baker," she amended her statement. "Saturday is my busiest day."

Kurt shifted his eyes to the rear-view mirror to look at Noelle as she sat in the extended cab of his truck. "I think somebody would love to stick her nose out the window. Do you mind if I roll them down in the back?"

"Just halfway," Clara said. "I don't want her falling out. Can you roll ours down, too? It's fun to ride with the wind in your face."

"You're not worried about your hair?"

"Not today, I'm not." Clara leaned toward her open window. The breeze scrambled her shoulder-length bob. "It's been years since I've done this. Something comes over me when we head to Bloom Cottage. It's as if I see the world through a softer lens. I'm focused on the moment and not worried about things that haven't happened yet."

"That's a great way to put it. I reconnect with the carefree boy I was years ago, and I leave feeling refreshed."

They turned off the highway onto the steep incline of the driveway to the cottage.

Clara held her breath. The house would be in full view when they crested the ridge ahead of them. Kurt would get his first glimpse of the swing. The construction supervisor had sent her a photo of it hanging on the porch. It looked exactly as she'd imagined. *Any second now.*

The truck leveled out at the top of the ridge. Kurt turned his eyes away from the house and pointed to a large concrete slab that hadn't been there when Clara had been at the cottage earlier that week to answer questions about the kitchen. "They got the garage slab poured," he said, pressing his foot to the brake as they drove past the house and stopped in front of the slab.

He got out of the truck and went to examine the floor of his new garage.

Clara climbed out of the passenger seat, and opened the rear door for Noelle to jump down. This wasn't what she'd imagined. Kurt was supposed to have seen the swing when they reached the house. He would cry out in surprise and glee, rush over to examine it, and take her into his arms as she'd followed in his wake. Noelle would leap for joy at their feet as he kissed her. That hadn't happened.

Clara joined him as he inspected the steel rebar sticking out of the concrete. She thought about suggesting that they enter the house by the front door, but that would be odd and a dead give-away that she was up to something. She'd convinced him to make the trip to the cottage to inspect the changes to the kitchen she'd authorized. They would enter the house by the back door for that. She'd have to find another way to get him onto the porch.

"With luck, they'll finish the garage before winter," he said, turning toward the house. "Let's see what you've done with the kitchen."

They entered through the back door. Clara explained the change she'd made to the placement of the island and showed him the installation of various pull-out shelves and organizers. She had him get down on his knees to confirm the placement of an electric outlet inside one of the lower cabinets.

"Why do I need a plug here?"

Clara demonstrated the shelf that swung out and up, locking into place. "You'll put your stand mixer here and plug it in there, so it's ready to use when you need it, without cluttering your countertop."

"That's cool. I've never used one of those big mixers and I don't have one, but I've seen Maisie's."

"You'll have to buy one." Clara grinned. "I'm available to shop for kitchen appliances and gadgets with you anytime. It's one of my favorite things to do."

"You're on," he said. He got to his feet and pulled her into his arms. "Thanks for designing such a beautiful kitchen for me. I would never have known to ask for any of this." He bent to kiss her.

She took a step back. "What was that?"

"I didn't hear anything."

"It was out front. Sort of a crash."

"I must be losing my hearing," Kurt said. "Maybe it's Noelle. She's running around out there."

"We'd better check," Clara said.

They crossed the living room to the front door.

Kurt threw it open, calling Noelle's name. He stepped over the threshold and froze.

Clara hovered behind him, standing on tiptoe to see over his shoulders.

The swing glowed in a swath of afternoon sunshine, its rich wood a warm golden brown. The glossy finish on its slats reflected the light.

"What?" Kurt moved to the swing like metal drawn to a magnet. A smile flooded his face and spilled down his frame until even his feet looked happy.

He ran his hands over the smooth wood, examining every joint. He gave it a gentle push and watched it swing in a graceful arch.

Clara stood a step behind, reveling in his obvious delight.

He turned to her. "You did this?"

She nodded.

He placed a hand on top of his head. "This is the surprise you didn't want to tell me about?"

"Yep. The man you saw me talking to is the woodworker who made this."

"Now I feel like a complete idiot all over again."

"None of that," Clara said in a tone that conveyed the topic wasn't up for discussion. "We've resolved it. The only thing I want you to feel now is happiness about your new swing."

"It's the most thoughtful gift I've ever received," he said, stopping the swing. He tugged on the chains, and when satisfied it was solid, he helped her into the swing. When she was situated, he took her face in his hands and kissed her tenderly.

"Sit," she said, patting the spot next to her. "Let's take this out for a test drive."

He settled next to her and pushed off to set the swing into motion.

They sat together and watched butterflies flit in the sunshine. Noelle zoomed in and out of the shadows. The sun warmed their faces.

Clara rested her head on his shoulder.

After a comfortable silence, he was the first to speak. "I need to double-check my photo, but I believe this is a replica of the swing my grandparents had."

"That's what I was going for," Clara said.

"I think the slats are the same size—and there are the same number of them. You've got an incredible memory for detail."

"Well… maybe not. I snuck a picture of that old photo of you on the swing and gave it to the woodworker. He had that to go on."

"Very clever. I'm impressed." He leaned in to kiss her again. "This is one thing I always wanted to do on that old swing, but never did."

They continued to canoodle until Noelle raced up the steps and leapt onto the swing, forcing them apart. Mud coated her paws and underbelly.

"Oh, Noelle. What have you gotten into?"

"One disadvantage of living close to a creek," Kurt said. "Muddy paws."

"We'd better clean her up," Clara said with a sigh. She didn't move. "I love sitting here, observing nature. This swing is magical. If this were mine, I'd start every day—with my coffee, my affirmations, and my prayers—right here on this swing."

A tsunami of emotion flooded through Kurt. He knew what he wanted—no, needed—to do. "Will you come here with me tomorrow? I'll pick you up at seven. We'll start our day here, on this swing." He didn't tell her that he hoped they'd start something more than just their day.

"Sure." She gave him a quizzical look. "You want to get up early on your day off?"

"You bet." He'd never wanted anything more, he thought. "Let's get this explorer cleaned up and head to Pinewood." He picked up the dog. "We've got dinner reservations at six-thirty."

Clara scooted off the swing, and they attended to Noelle.

Kurt dropped Clara off by mid afternoon.

She yawned as she and Noelle got out of his truck. "Excuse me," she said. "I'm going to take a nap." She looked at him with mock seriousness. "I'm never going to fall asleep on a date again."

He laughed.

"What will you do with the rest of your afternoon?"

He shrugged. "This and that." *If she only knew the number of stops he needed to make before they returned to the swing in the morning.*

CHAPTER 28

The sun poked in and out of the trees as it made its way toward its zenith the following morning. The porch was still in the shade when Kurt and Clara arrived.

Kurt had arrived at Bloom Cottage before dawn, with armloads of flowers he'd purchased the previous day right before closing from the downtown florist. The champagne and orange juice he'd bought at the 24-hour grocery sat in ice buckets on the porch floor. Maisie had been delighted to let him borrow champagne flutes.

He'd brought his elaborate espresso maker from home and set it up in the kitchen, together with his favorite rechargeable mugs that kept coffee hot for hours.

The only inelegant part of his plan was the bucket of donut holes he'd bought at a drive-through donut shop. He knew she secretly loved them and hoped she'd be pleased.

Roses, hydrangeas, and daisies festooned the arms of the swing and the chains holding it up. Attaching flowers to the swing had proved harder than he'd thought. He'd eventually been successful using zip ties. He'd trimmed away any long tails and hid the ties among the foliage.

His final touch had been to trail rose petals across the porch and down the steps.

He sped up past the house and parked by the back door.

"You came in hot." Clara teased as the truck came to a stop.

"My coffee maker is inside," he said. "We'll take our cups out to the swing."

Clara turned to him, a surprised look on her face. "When did you do that? There wasn't a coffee machine here yesterday."

He ignored her question and escorted her into the kitchen.

"Your usual?" he asked.

She nodded and sidled over to the kitchen window. "This is a beautiful view, too. Let's face it—Bloom Cottage doesn't have a bad side."

He held a mug out to her, and she took it from him, inhaling the aroma of the steaming liquid. "There's nothing like hot coffee in the morning."

He smiled and picked up his cup.

They walked to the front door. He hesitated before he unlocked it. "Let me take that from you," he said. "I'll hand it back when you're in the swing."

"I can manage my cup with one hand without spilling," she said.

He took the cup from her, nonetheless, and placed it with his on the floor by the door.

Clara narrowed her eyes. What was wrong with him this morning?

He opened the door and stepped aside.

The sight that greeted her answered her question. She brought her right hand to her throat and turned to him.

Kurt led Clara across the rose petals to the swing. She sat at the edge, keeping her feet on the floor to prevent it from moving.

Kurt dropped to one knee and reached for her right hand. "Clara Conway, I've been in love with you since the first time we met. You're the kindest, most honorable person I've ever known.

I want to spend my life at your side, seeing the world through your joyful filter. When I take photos on this swing, I want you to be in every one of them."

Her tears splashed onto their clasped hands. He reached up and brushed them from her cheek with his thumb.

"I've been wanting this—yearning for this—in my heart for a very long time. We don't know what the future will bring. I realized last night that the only thing I'm certain of is that I want to spend the rest of my days with you." He kissed her hand. "Will you marry me?"

Clara grasped his arm and pulled him to her. "Yes." The words escaped between her tears. "I love you, Kurt. I'd be honored to be your wife and go through this journey with you. You inspire me and see the best in me."

They kissed, and cried, and dried each other's tears.

Kurt opened the champagne and made them each a mimosa.

They toasted their dreams of a future together as the sun came over the top of the house and the porch was bathed in sunshine.

"Do you want your coffee?" Kurt asked. "It'll still be hot."

"You are the perfect man," she said.

"I figured we'd be hungry, so I have donut holes."

Clara shrieked. "And I didn't think you could get any better! Let's have them."

Kurt retrieved the bucket and fed Clara a powdered sugar donut hole.

"Mmmm…" she moaned as she chewed.

"I want you to have a ring, of course," he said, licking sugar off of his fingers. "You'll have to pick it out. I don't know anything about diamonds."

"I'm ready and able to sign up for that mission," she teased.

"When do you want to go shopping?"

"I think the downtown jeweler opens at nine tomorrow." She arched a brow at him.

"It just so happens I don't have anything on my calendar until noon. I'll pick you up at eight forty-five."

Clara leaned her head against the back of the swing and inhaled deeply. "I can't believe this is happening." She looked at Kurt. "I also can't imagine living my life any other way than by your side."

Kurt kissed her again, and time slipped away.

"Who should we tell first?" he asked, tracing his finger along the side of her face.

"Maisie already knows," Clara said. "I recognize her champagne flutes."

"I can't slip anything by you, can I? I'll have to remember that. She knew I was going to propose, but she didn't know if you'd accept."

Clara rolled her eyes. "She knew I'd accept. Let's go to see them after lunch." She popped the last donut hole in her mouth and drained her coffee. "Noelle. I think Noelle has to be the first to know."

Kurt chuckled. "Then Noelle it will be. Before we go, I want to return to something we were doing earlier."

He leaned in, she slipped her arms around his neck, and their lips met.

THE END

THANK YOU FOR READING

If you enjoyed Tarts & Turnovers, I'd be grateful if you wrote a review.

Just a few lines on Amazon or Goodreads would be great. Reviews are the best gift an author can receive. They encourage us when they're good, help us improve our next book when they're not, and help other readers make informed choices when purchasing books. Goodreads reviews help readers find new books. Reviews on Amazon keep the Amazon algorithms humming and are the most helpful aide in selling books! Thank you.

To post a review on Amazon:

1. Go to the product detail page for Tarts & Turnovers on Amazon.com.

2. Click "Write a customer review" in the Customer Reviews section.

3. Write your review and click Submit.

In gratitude,
Barbara Hinske

ACKNOWLEDGMENTS

I'm blessed with the wisdom and support of many kind and generous people. I want to thank the most supportive and delightful group of champions an author could hope for:

My remarkable husband, Brian Willis, who never fails to steer me in the right direction when I'm stuck on a plot point;

My life coach Mat Boggs for your wisdom and guidance;

My kind and generous legal team, Kenneth Kleinberg, Esq., and Michael McCarthy—thank you for believing in my vision;

The professional "dream team" of my editors Linden Gross, Kelly Byrd, and proofreader Dana Lee;

Elizabeth Mackey for a beautiful cover.

ABOUT THE AUTHOR

USA Today Bestselling and Amazon All Star Author BARBARA HINSKE is an attorney and novelist. She loves to read and write women's fiction, mystery/thriller/suspense, and sweet Christmas stories. She's authored the Guiding Emily series, the mystery thriller collection "Who's There?", the Paws & Pastries series, three of the novellas in The Wishing Tree series, and the beloved Rosemont series. Her novella *The Christmas Club* and novel *Guiding Emily* have both been adapted for the Hallmark Channel.

ENJOY THIS EXCERPT FROM GUIDING EMILY

Prologue

Emily. The woman who would become everything to me. The person I would eat every meal with and lie down next to every night—for the rest of my days.

She was just ahead; behind that door at the far end of the long hall. I glanced over my shoulder. Mark kept pace, slightly behind me. I could feel his excitement. It matched my own.

Everyone said Emily and I would be perfect for each other. I'd overheard them talking when they thought I was asleep. I spend a lot of time with my eyes closed, but I don't sleep much. They didn't know that.

"A magical match," they'd all agreed.

I lifted my eyes to Mark, and he nodded his encouragement. I gave a brief shake of my head. Only four more doorways between Emily and me.

I picked up my pace. A cylindrical orange object on the carpet in the third doorway from the end caught my eye. *Is that a Cheeto? A Crunchy Cheeto? I love Crunchy Cheetos.*

I tore my eyes away.

This was no time to get distracted.

We sped across the remaining distance to the doorway at the end of the hall. The door that separated me from my destiny.

I froze and waited while Mark knocked.

I heard Emily's voice—the sound I would come to love above all others—say, "Come in."

What was that in her voice? Eagerness—anxiety—maybe even a touch of fear? I'd take care of all of that right away.

The door swung open and Mark stepped back. He pointed to Emily.

I'd seen her before. Emily Main was a beautiful young woman in her late twenties. Auburn hair cascaded around her shoulders and shone like a new penny. With my jet-black coloring, we'd make a striking couple.

"Go on," Mark said.

I abandoned all my training—all sense of decorum—and raced to her.

Emily reached for me and flung her arms around my neck.

I placed my nose against her throat, and she tumbled out of her chair onto her knees.

I swept my tongue over her cheek, tasting the saltiness of her tears.

"Oh … Garth." My name on her lips came out in a hoarse whisper.

I wagged my tail so hard that we both lay back on the floor.

"Good boy, Garth!"

She rubbed the ridge of my skull behind my ears in a way that would become one of my favorite things in the whole wide world.

Next to food.

Especially Crunchy Cheetos.

Mark and the other trainers were right—we were made for each other. I was the perfect guide dog for Emily Main.

Chapter 1

"Weren't you supposed to leave for the airport half an hour ago?" Michael Ward asked his boss, whose fingers were typing furiously on her keyboard. "You're still planning to get married, aren't you?"

Emily Main's head bobbed behind the computer, her eyes fixed to the screen.

"I can't believe you put off a departure to Fiji to help us launch this new program. Your wedding's in two days."

"We've been working on this for almost a year. I wasn't about to leave when we're this close. I just need to finish this last email." She hunched forward and peered at the computer screen.

"There," she said, pushing her office chair back as the email *whooshed* from her inbox. "Done."

She looked up at Michael, blinking. It was probably the first time she had looked at anything besides a computer screen in hours. "I brought my suitcase so I could go to the airport straight from the office. I don't have to stop at home."

Michael raised his eyebrows at her. "That's all you've got? A carry-on and a satchel for a week—a week that includes your wedding? My wife packs more than that for a three-day weekend."

"My wedding dress is a classic sheath and the rest is bathing suits and shorts."

"I would have thought Connor Harrington the third would have wanted an elaborate wedding—one fit for the society pages."

"Our wedding is going to be very elegant—think JFK Junior and Carolyn," Emily said, flinging her purse over her shoulder and reaching for the retractable handle of her suitcase.

Michael stepped in front of her. "I've got this," he said. "I'll walk you to the street. I'd like to congratulate Connor on snagging our office hero."

Emily hesitated.

"He is picking you up, isn't he? You're flying there together?"

"He went out over the weekend. He wanted to do some diving

with his best man … sort of a bachelor party reprise. I was traveling with my mom and maid of honor, but they flew out yesterday as planned. The company paid to change my ticket, but it would have cost almost five hundred dollars for Mom and Gina to change theirs. It wasn't worth it."

"But you don't like to fly." He peered into Emily's face. "Did you talk to Connor about that before you decided to stay an extra day? You have told him about your fear of flying, haven't you?"

Emily shrugged. "I've mentioned it, sure, but I haven't made a big deal out of it."

"So what did he say?"

"He suggested that I get a prescription for Xanax and sleep the whole way out there."

"Really? That's what he said?"

"He's a Brit, for heaven's sake. 'Stiff upper lip' and all that. He's not the sort of guy to coddle anyone—and I'm not a needy type of gal. You know that."

Michael cocked his head to one side. "Do you have to change planes?"

Emily nodded.

"You don't want to be knocked out for that."

"I'll be fine." Emily threw her shoulders back. "You don't need to worry about me."

"I know—I'm sorry. It's just that I wouldn't let my wife make the trip alone if she felt like you do about flying."

"I fly alone all the time, and nothing's ever happened to me. There's no reason this time should be any different."

Michael lifted his hands, palms facing her, and shrugged. "Okay, but I think he could have at least offered to pay to change your mom's flight or something."

"I'll be perfectly fine." Emily walked past him into the hallway. "I promised Dhruv that I'd say goodbye before I leave."

"He's going to miss you. You're the one person here that really connects with him."

Michael watched her shoulders sag slightly.

"Hey," he said, rolling the carry-on to a halt beside her in the hall. "I'm sorry. I didn't mean to worry you. The whole team is going to step into your shoes while you're gone. We've talked about it."

"Of course you will. I shouldn't worry about him. I've got the best team in San Francisco. Scratch that. On the entire West Coast." Emily gave him a teary smile and punched him playfully on the shoulder. "I know you'll take care of everything while I'm away, Michael—including helping Dhruv stay connected with the team."

"Good!" Michael continued down the hallway. "I don't want you to give this place a second thought while you're gone. If anyone deserves a vacation—and a gorgeous beach wedding—it's you, Em. But don't get too comfortable." Michael turned and smiled at her. "We do need you to come back. We'd be lost without you here."

Emily laughed and pushed him toward the elevator. "Why don't you go push that button, you wonderful suck-up. It'll take ages to get an elevator this time of the morning. I'll stick my head into Dhruv's cubicle and be right back."

***

Emily found Dhruv, as usual, leaning into the bank of computer monitors, intently focused on the complex strings of code in front of him. She cleared her throat. When Dhruv didn't move, she tapped him lightly on the shoulder.

Dhruv sat back quickly and spun around. A smile spread across his face when he saw her.

"I wanted to say goodbye before I go."

Dhruv nodded. "Goodbye."

"I'll see you a week from Monday."

"I know. You're getting married in two days, then you have

your honeymoon for a week, then you come back to work," he recited.

"That's right. You remembered."

"I remember things."

"Yes, you do. That's one reason you're so very good at programming," she said.

"I know."

"Okay … well … have a good week. You can go to Michael if you have … if you need anything."

"I know."

Emily regarded the shy, socially awkward middle-aged man who was, by far, the most proficient member of her extremely talented team of programmers. "Bye."

Dhruv nodded.

Emily stepped away.

Dhruv leapt out of his chair and called after her. "Have a happy wedding."

Emily swung around and gave him a thumbs-up then turned back toward the elevators where Michael was waiting.

From *Guiding Emily*

CONNECT WITH BARBARA HINSKE ONLINE

Sign up for her newsletter at **BarbaraHinske.com**
    Goodreads.com/BarbaraHinske
    Facebook/bhinske
    Instagram/barbarahinskeauthor
    TikTok.com/BarbaraHinske
    Pinterest.com/BarbaraHinske
    X.com/BarbaraHinske
    Search for **Barbara Hinske on YouTube**
    bhinske@gmail.com

Novels in the Guiding Emily Series

Guiding Emily (adapted for The Hallmark Channel, 2023)

The Unexpected Path

Over Every Hurdle

Down the Aisle

From the Heart

Novels in the "Who's There?!" Collection

Deadly Parcel

Final Circuit